# INTERNAL MEMO

TO:     All staff
FROM: Victoria Colby
RE:     Love in the Workplace

I am proud to announce that many of
our colleagues have recently tied the knot.
I'd like to think that the Colby Agency is
responsible for the latest crop of wedding
announcements! Please join me in celebrating
the nuptials of Katherine Roertson and
Jack Raine, Nick Foster and Laura Proctor,
Ian Michaels and Nicole Reed, Trevor Sloan
and Rachel Larson, Rick Martinez and
Piper Ryan, Alex Preston and Mitch Hayden,
and Zach Ashton and Elizabeth McCormick.

Who will be next?

Dear Harlequin Intrigue Reader,

The suspenseful tales we offer you this month are much scarier than Halloween's ghouls and ghosts! So bring out your trick-or-treating bag and gather up all four exciting stories.

And do we have a *treat* for you—a brand-new 3-in-1 compilation featuring authors Rebecca York, Ann Voss Peterson and Patricia Rosemoor. Ten years ago, three men were cursed by a Gypsy woman bent on vengeance. Now they must race to find a killer—and true love's kiss may just break the evil spell they're under in *Gypsy Magic*.

Next, Aimée Thurlo concludes her two-book miniseries SIGN OF THE GRAY WOLF, with *Navajo Justice*. And Susan Kearney starts a new trilogy, THE CROWN AFFAIR, in which royalty of the country of Vashmira must battle palace danger and treachery, while finding true love along the way. Look for *Royal Target* this month.

When Jennifer Ballard dreamed of her wedding day, it never included murder! But no one would harm the beautiful bride, not if Colby Agency investigator Ethan Delaney had anything to say about it. Pick up *Contract Bride* for yet another nail-biter from Debra Webb.

Happy reading!

Denise O'Sullivan
Associate Senior Editor
Harlequin Intrigue

# CONTRACT BRIDE
## DEBRA WEBB

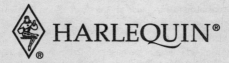

# HARLEQUIN®

TORONTO • NEW YORK • LONDON
AMSTERDAM • PARIS • SYDNEY • HAMBURG
STOCKHOLM • ATHENS • TOKYO • MILAN • MADRID
PRAGUE • WARSAW • BUDAPEST • AUCKLAND

ISBN 0-373-22683-7

CONTRACT BRIDE

## ABOUT THE AUTHOR

Debra Webb was born in Scottsboro, Alabama, to parents who taught her that anything is possible if you want it badly enough. She began writing at age nine. Eventually she met and married the man of her dreams and tried some other occupations, including selling vacuum cleaners, working in a factory, a day-care center, a hospital and a department store. When her husband joined the military, they moved to Berlin, Germany, and Debra became a secretary in the commanding general's office. By 1985 they were back in the States, and they finally moved to Tennessee, to a small town where everyone knows everyone else. With the support of her husband and two beautiful daughters, Debra took up writing again, looking to mystery and movies for inspiration. In 1998 her dream of writing for Harlequin came true. You can write to Debra with your comments at P.O. Box 64, Huntland, Tennessee 37345.

## Books by Debra Webb

HARLEQUIN INTRIGUE
583—SAFE BY HIS SIDE*
597—THE BODYGUARD'S BABY*
610—PROTECTIVE CUSTODY*
634—SPECIAL ASSIGNMENT: BABY
646—SOLITARY SOLDIER*
659—PERSONAL PROTECTOR*
671—PHYSICAL EVIDENCE*
683—CONTRACT BRIDE*

*Colby Agency

HARLEQUIN AMERICAN ROMANCE
864—LONGWALKER'S CHILD
935—THE MARRIAGE PRESCRIPTION*

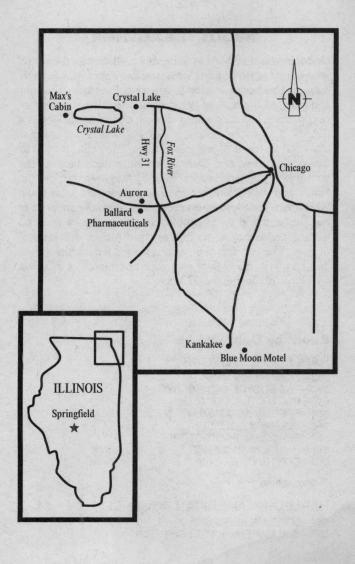

# CAST OF CHARACTERS

*Jennifer Ballard*—The daughter of pharmaceuticals magnate Austin Ballard. Who is she really? She can't seem to prove her true identity, but one thing is certain...someone wants her dead.

*Ethan Delaney*—Former Special Forces soldier turned Colby Agency investigator. If anyone can prove the identity of the real Jennifer Ballard, it's Ethan. But can he keep her safe and not lose his heart, as he has sworn he will never again do?

*Victoria Colby*—The head of the Colby Agency.

*David Crane*—A vice president at Ballard Pharmaceuticals and the fiancé of the real Jennifer Ballard. Is Crane friend or foe? After all, he did once save Ethan's life.

*Dr. Kessler*—The genius behind a new, revolutionary cancer drug. Is he simply out for revenge against Ballard Pharmaceuticals?

*Lucas Camp*—The deputy director of a highly covert government organization. A very good friend of Victoria Colby's.

*John Logan*—A specialist in Lucas's organization.

*Simon Ruhl*—One of the Colby Agency's finest.

*Amy Wells*—A receptionist at the Colby Agency.

This book is dedicated to the kind of friend who doesn't come along very often. A lady with whom you can share your hopes and dreams and, most important, your accomplishments. But more than anything she has been there for me—always. She has been my cheerleader, my confidante and my advisor. I can never thank her enough. This one is for you, Lyn Stone. For all your kind words and understanding, for all your praise and faith...for being a true friend.

# Prologue

Jennifer Ballard stared at her reflection in the cheval mirror once more, anticipation swirling inside her. A veil of French netting draped her shoulders and the exquisite headpiece adorned her upswept blond hair. The fitted bodice of her gown was heavily embellished with pearl and sequin detailing and the flowing satin skirt and chapel-length train were the stuff of which Cinderella-dreams were made.

She drew in a deep, calming breath. This was her wedding day—the day she'd waited for her entire life.

She'd always dreamed of a wedding exactly like this. A fairy-tale chapel set upon a wooded hillside…a handsome groom who would love and protect her from this day forward. Though much older than she, David Crane was both kind and compassionate. She respected him personally as well as professionally. He didn't quite make her heart go pitter-patter, but there was much more to life than that. He understood her, respected her work, and more important, her father trusted him implicitly.

*Her father.* A fresh wave of tears brimmed. If only

he was well enough to be here, but he wasn't. He'd insisted she not delay her wedding for him. Instead, he'd asked his old friend, Russell Gardner, to be his stand-in and give her away. Jenn smiled a little at that. She loved Russell, too. She'd called him Uncle Russ for as long as she could remember. If her father couldn't give her away, there was no one else she would prefer to do the honor.

The sound of the dressing-room door opening startled Jenn from her musings. She turned to see who'd violated the strict rule that no one was to see the bride until the wedding march sounded.

She smiled in spite of herself. "Uncle Russ, what—?"

He lunged, half stumbling, across the tiny room and grabbed her by the shoulders. "You must run, Jenn. Run as far and as fast as you can."

Worry stole into her heart. "I don't understand. Has something happened to my father?"

Russ shook her hard. "Listen to me," he said hoarsely. "Run!"

Only then did Jenn notice the pallor of his complexion, and the tiny beads of sweat forming on his brow. "What's wrong? Tell me what's happened?"

"It's Crane," he said tightly, as if it pained him to speak. "You mustn't believe anything he says. He's lied…" A strangled groan rendered the rest of his words unintelligible.

"What are you saying?" She couldn't have heard him right. She knew David. He would never lie, certainly not to her. Russ tried to continue, but swayed as if too weak to stand. She steadied him. "Please tell me what's wrong!"

"The Kessler Project. There's something very... wrong," he murmured. "He's lied about all of it. Your life is in grave danger...there are things you don't know..."

His knees buckled and he collapsed in Jenn's arms. "Oh, God!" She staggered beneath his weight as she lowered him to the floor. He was unconscious. She started to shake him, but the bright crimson stain painted down the front of her dress captured her attention.

*Blood.*

Now, with the lapels of his tuxedo jacket flared open, she could see that Russ was bleeding. She stared down at his still form, shock settling over her. A small round hole in his chest was steadily leaking the dark life-giving fluid.

He'd been shot.

Commanding herself to act, she checked his pulse. Her own heart pounded. Her fingers shook with fear. No pulse.

Dear God, she had to get help.

"He's in here."

Jenn's head snapped up at the sound of David's voice. She hadn't even realized he'd come in. Three of his friends followed. Had something happened outside? Something she hadn't heard? Thank God he was here.

*David would help.*

"Russ needs an ambulance!" she shouted, hot tears

streaming down her cheeks. *Please,* she prayed, *make them hurry.*

"Get him out of here," David directed.

Two of David's friends picked up a deathly still Russ and started for the door.

"What are they doing?" Jenn asked, a new kind of terror welling in her chest. "Where are they taking him? Someone needs to be doing CPR. He isn't..."

David just looked at her, his eyes completely empty of emotion.

She pushed to her feet. Her knees wobbled. The whole scene felt surreal...like a nightmare. This couldn't be happening. "Didn't you hear me?" she demanded of her fiancé. "He needs help. He's dying!"

David adjusted the jacket of his elegant tux, then turned to the man at his side. "Kill her."

# Chapter One

"No," Ethan Delaney said firmly. "I don't do freelance work. You'll have to find yourself another man."

The man on the other end of the line pulled out all the stops with a last-ditch effort to persuade him to reconsider. The offer jumped to a cool million.

Ethan just shook his head. Anyone who offered that much money was likely up to no good. Especially since they wanted to keep the mission hush-hush and refused to go to the police. Retrieving a supposedly kidnapped relative from a third-world country where drugs were the number-one export was just plain asking for trouble.

"Good day, Mr. Santiago," Ethan said, then hung up.

Some people just couldn't take no for an answer. Ethan was a Colby agent. He took his assignments from one person and one person only. Victoria Colby. Of course, most of the time those orders were passed along to him by Ian Michaels, her second in command. But Ethan didn't mind that. He liked Ian. Ethan grinned. He liked the guy's wife even better. Nicole was really something. She worked at the Colby Agency now, as well, in research mostly. Ian didn't want the mother of his child doing fieldwork. Ethan couldn't blame him. If he had a woman like that, he'd take good care of her, too.

But that wasn't going to happen. He would never allow himself to get that close to another human being again. Nowadays he kept things simple…uncomplicated.

A light tap on his office door drew Ethan's attention in that direction. Amy Wells smiled at him before stepping inside.

"Hey, Ethan," she said as she placed a couple of reports in his inbox. She was young…very young. Only twenty-three, if memory served him right. And about as naive as they came. "Mildred asked me to drop off the reports Victoria signed."

He leaned back in his chair and gifted the Colby Agency's receptionist with a high-voltage smile. "Good morning, Amy. I appreciate you delivering those personally."

That was all it took. She blushed and immediately started to back out of his office. "Have a nice day."

"It would be a lot nicer if you'd agree to have lunch with me," he suggested, knowing full well what her reaction would be.

Her eyes rounded. "I—I…ah…think I'll probably have to work right through lunch."

He shook his head solemnly and blew out a breath as if weary of her rejections. "That's a shame."

"Gotta go!" she almost squeaked.

Ethan chuckled as he watched her all but fly from his

office. Her answer was the same every time. The kid was afraid of her shadow and considered him to be some sort of bogeyman. He loved to tease her.

The intercom on his desk buzzed and he pressed the speaker button. "Delaney here."

"Ethan, could you come to my office, please."

*Victoria.* "Sure thing." He pushed back from his desk and stood. "On my way."

Ethan left his office and strolled down the richly carpeted corridor. He winked at Amy as he passed the arched entryway that led to the vacant reception area. She abruptly looked away, color rising in her cheeks once more.

Elegantly appointed furnishings and tasteful decorating lent the perfect ambiance to the prestigious agency. From the moment a prospective client entered those polished mahogany doors, there was never any question as to the caliber of the staff housed here. But as on most Mondays, it was quiet.

The Colby Agency was the best in the business of private investigations and personal protection. No one even got close to matching Victoria Colby's stellar reputation. She had clients from all over the world. She had a staff of highly qualified, handpicked investigators.

That had been the thing that made Ethan take a second look when she had recruited him. At thirty-one, and only eight years from retirement, he'd walked away from his military career without a backward glance. He clenched his jaw, purposely pushing those thoughts aside. One year later, Victoria had wanted him on her team. At the interview, she'd said that he had come highly recommended by some friend of hers who had military connections. Lucas Camp—whoever he was. Though Ethan had never met him, he knew from Victoria's description that Camp was one of those top-secret spooks that weren't supposed to exist. There probably weren't more than a handful of people alive who knew who Lucas Camp was and what he did. Obviously, Victoria was one of the chosen few. Ethan only knew the rumors.

Twenty-fours hours after the first meeting between Ethan and Victoria, he had accepted her offer. The salary was outstanding, but that's not what had sold him on the Colby Agency. Case in point, this morning's telephone call. Not even a million dollars could buy Ethan Delaney if he didn't want to be bought.

Honesty and loyalty were the two qualities that mattered most to him. Victoria didn't play games and she never, ever allowed herself or her people to be manipulated. Victoria Colby was the genuine article. Straight as an arrow and completely loyal.

She thoroughly investigated every client who walked through those doors. Ethan didn't have to worry about being used or set up. He intended personally to insure that that never happened again. Those haunting memories from the past tried to surface once more. He banished them instantly.

It was over. He couldn't change the past. But he could damn well prevent history from repeating itself.

Ethan paused in Victoria's doorway. She was alone. He'd fully expected to find Ian there as well. "Morning, Victoria."

"Good morning, Ethan. Please come in and have a seat." She gestured to one of the two wingback chairs that flanked her desk. "I have a possible new client I'd like to discuss with you."

"Great." Ethan settled into one of the chairs, thankful for a new assignment. He preferred to stay busy and since he'd completed his last case over a week ago, he was getting a little antsy. "I can be ready to go wherever and whenever you need me—today would be terrific." *The sooner the better,* he almost added.

Victoria smiled. "That's one of the things I like about you, Ethan. Your enthusiasm for your work."

Ethan nodded, acknowledging the compliment. He'd come really close to going in the other direction just before Victoria found him. Three years ago, his last military mission had almost cost him his ability to care, as well as his life. But the Colby Agency had given both back to him.

He was whole again.

For the most part, anyway.

Victoria relaxed into her leather chair and studied him for a moment. It was her way. He'd gotten used to the reflective moments she indulged in. He simply sat back and enjoyed the view. She was a very attractive woman, even at fifty. Her hair was still raven, with just a few threads of gray and she had the darkest eyes. The kind that could see right through to the heart of things. Honest eyes. That lovely face, however, was not without its share of hard-earned lines. Lines that spoke of experience and loss.

Though Ethan didn't know the whole story, he'd

heard the talk. Victoria's husband had been murdered. That devastating event had come only five years after the loss of her seven-year-old son. She never talked about that either. Only two people knew the whole story—Mildred, her personal secretary, assistant really, and Trevor Sloan, a former Colby investigator. But everyone had heard the talk.

Victoria Colby had suffered more than her fair share of pain. But it seemed only to make her stronger...more determined to make the world right in any way she could.

"I'm sure you're familiar with Ballard Pharmaceuticals, better known as BalPhar, down in Aurora."

Ethan recognized the name. "They're one of our long-term clients." The company was well known for its headline-making research, he recalled. When it came to pioneering new drugs, BalPhar was a leader in the industry.

"The Colby Agency has done business with Austin Ballard for more than ten years," Victoria went on. "We've done the background clearance on all his employees and the occasional investigation into companies with whom they were considering doing business. I have a great deal of respect for Austin. That's the main reason I'm considering taking this case in spite of the suspicious circumstances."

"I thought Simon took care of BalPhar's work," Ethan countered. Simon Ruhl was former FBI. No one was better at digging up dirt on people and companies than Simon. Ethan definitely didn't want to horn in on his territory.

"That's true, but he's on an assignment that he can't break away from at the moment. I believe that time is of the essence where this case is concerned."

Ethan frowned. That sounded a little ominous. "What's the deal?"

"Austin has a twenty-two-year-old daughter, Jennifer. She's something of a genius. Graduated high school by thirteen, had her doctorate by the time she was eighteen. She's worked side by side with her father since she was a child. Every moment she wasn't in school, she was in a lab."

Ethan immediately pictured big, thick eyeglasses and hair pulled into a bun. Oh yeah, and the proverbial white lab coat. "She sounds like an interesting lady." *To a microscope,* he added to himself.

A tiny smile disrupted Victoria's usually all-business expression. "I'm sure you'll find her most interesting, especially under the circumstances."

He shrugged. "So what's her problem?"

"She thinks someone is trying to kill her."

The blunt statement jerked Ethan to a higher level of attention. "Someone?"

"She believes the threat to her life is coming from inside her father's company."

A frown nagged at Ethan. "What does her father say about it?"

"He's gravely ill," she explained. "His medical problem started more than a year ago. But about six months ago he became bedridden. My understanding of his current condition is that he drifts in and out of a catatonic state. He may not even be aware of his daughter's claims.''

"Where's Miss Ballard now?''

"In hiding. She gave me a location where she can be found. She'd like to meet with someone as soon as possible.''

The skepticism in Victoria's voice was impossible to miss. "You don't trust her?'' Ethan asked.

Victoria sighed. "I don't know her. My contact prior to this has been strictly with her father. We have a couple of news clippings of her with her father in the file, none of which are very good pictures. A little too fuzzy. But there is one photograph that was taken five years ago. Austin has kept her pretty much shielded from the press. She is his only child and he's been more than a little overprotective. Which, in that cutthroat business, makes a great deal of sense.''

"Something doesn't sit right with you,'' Ethan suggested. He could sense her hesitation.

Victoria considered his statement for a moment. "This agency has investigated every single employee at BalPhar. They're all clean. Of course that doesn't mean that one hasn't gone bad.'' She paused and chose her words carefully when she spoke once more. "I think my hesitation has more to do with the daughter's past and her reluctance to share details than with anything else.''

Ethan lifted an eyebrow. "Now you've really got my interest.''

"As I said before,'' Victoria went on. "She's brilliant. But with that level of brilliance come other problems. Social, sometimes emotional. She's led a very sheltered life. I remember there was a problem in her final semester of undergraduate school. A breakdown of some sort. It didn't last long and probably had more to do with her young age than anything else. According to Austin she was back on her feet and ready to dive into graduate courses in no time. But still, with the continued decline in his health, this new development gives me pause.''

Ethan could see what she meant. If the lady had any history of emotional instability, then the weight of her father's illness might be more than she could bear. ''Is she running the company in his absence?''

Victoria sighed. ''Yes. She's senior vice president. A breakdown on her part could be disastrous for BalPhar during this critical time. The shareholders and benefactors Austin has worked a lifetime to develop will be monitoring every move she makes very closely. Do you see my concern?''

''I definitely do. That's a lot of responsibility for someone so young, genius or not.''

''Exactly.'' Victoria shook her head. ''And, if I had my guess, emotionally and socially she's far younger than twenty-two. I'm relatively certain she hasn't led a typical lifestyle in any sense of the word.''

Something Victoria had said nagged at Ethan. ''You said senior vice president, is there more than one?''

''Yes,'' Victoria hastened to explain. ''I ran a brief check on the company's current status this morning. Dr. David Crane is the second vice president. As Austin's daughter, Jennifer outranks him, of course.''

*David Crane.* Ethan knew a moment of disbelief. The kind a guy felt when he thought he'd seen a ghost. Crane was a ghost, all right. One straight from Ethan's past.

"What does Crane say about all this?" he asked hesitantly. Flashes of memory slashed through his brain. Gunfire erupting, running, death hot on their heels. He blinked the images away.

Victoria eyed him curiously, noting his brief distraction. She never missed a thing. "I haven't spoken with Dr. Crane. I promised Jennifer that I would not contact anyone at the company or the local authorities until we'd looked into her accusations. Which, of course, we can't actually do until she gives us more details and Jennifer won't do that until she's met with you face-to-face." Victoria inclined her head and studied Ethan for another moment. "Do you know Dr. Crane?"

Ethan considered saying no, but he wouldn't lie to his boss. Avoiding the truth was something he only did when absolutely necessary. "I knew him. In another lifetime."

"Should we be suspicious of him?"

Ethan shook his head. "I don't think so. He saved my life in Iraq. He seemed a pretty straight arrow."

"I see. He was in the military at the same time as you?"

"No," Ethan said, still distracted by this unexpected development. "He was a scientist being held hostage. I went in to retrieve him. On the way out, he watched my back, kept me from taking a bullet."

"Perhaps I should ask someone else to look into this

case then," she offered. "I don't want anything getting in the way of objectivity. If there's any chance Jennifer is right in her claims, Crane may come under suspicion."

Ethan put up his hands, stop-sign fashion. "Don't sweat it. Crane and I haven't seen each other in nearly a decade. Besides, we don't even know that Miss Ballard thinks he's involved. But, even if he is, ancient history won't color my judgment, I can assure you."

Several tense seconds ticked by while Victoria weighed his words. Caution was her first line of defense. "All right," she said, finally relenting. "But if your past with Crane gets in the way, I expect you to bow out gracefully."

"That's reasonable," he allowed. "What do you want me to do?" The girl sounded like she needed help, and things could definitely get sticky whether Crane was involved or not. Ethan would have to evaluate the situation closely before coming to any kind of conclusions. The reputation of a pharmaceuticals company was fragile. One wrong move and years of research, not to mention millions of dollars, could end up down the drain. New, badly needed drugs could be delayed in reaching those who needed them now.

"She's given me the name of a motel in Kankakee, a small town about fifty miles south of Chicago. I want you to talk to her. Determine if there's any possibility that her claims are valid."

"And if they aren't?" Ethan had to know what was expected of him if the girl had gone around the bend.

"Check out her story and if it's clear to you that she's

unstable, then somehow we'll have Dr. Melbourne take a look at her before we do anything else. I don't want to risk bad press unnecessarily. With Austin's illness already a matter of public knowledge, this sort of thing could ruin all that he's worked for.''

''What if she doesn't want to see Melbourne?'' Ethan remembered the doc well from his prehiring interviews. The guy was a genius himself. If there was anything even slightly off-kilter, he'd find it. Melbourne was good—the best.

''Well, then we'll just have to find a way to convince her.'' Victoria looked him straight in the eye. ''Discounting what you've just told me about your past with Crane, I chose you for this mission for two reasons, Ethan.''

He held that all-knowing gaze and waited for her to continue.

''If there is any truth to her accusations, I want her protected at all costs. I won't take any chances with Austin's daughter. Secondly, your powers of persuasion where the ladies are concerned have not gone unnoticed. I'm certain you can convince Miss Ballard to see things your way.''

Ethan grinned. ''I'll do my best.''

''I'm sure you will.'' Victoria leaned forward and handed him a folded piece of paper. ''That's the location. I'm to call her at the number she left and let her know whom to expect. She would like to meet with you at one o'clock this afternoon. Does that give you time to prepare?''

''I can handle it.'' It was nine a.m. He'd have plenty

of time to go by his apartment and pick up a few things just in case this assignment took more than twenty-four hours. He tucked the note into his pocket. "I'll call you the moment I have anything to report."

"Very good."

Ethan headed to the door, mentally making a list of what he would need.

"Just one more thing," Victoria called behind him.

He paused at the door and looked back. "Yeah?"

"Since I don't know Jennifer personally, there's always the chance that this young woman is an impostor attempting to cause trouble for BalPhar. Maybe a disgruntled ex-employee seeking revenge. She could be a threat to security."

"That's possible," Ethan agreed.

"Whatever you discover, do not let this woman out of your sight. If she's Jennifer Ballard, I want her protected. If she's not, I want to ensure she represents no threat to the real Jennifer. We'll need to inform BalPhar security as soon as there are any firm facts."

"I won't let anything happen to her either way."

Ethan left Victoria's office with uneasiness twisting in his gut. Something about this whole thing didn't feel right. Victoria felt it, too, that was the reason for the extra precautions. A dread, at once familiar and disconcerting, filtered through him. He'd been in this kind of situation where there were far too many variables once before. That situation had ended badly and almost cost him his life.

He wouldn't let his guard down this time. No matter how sweet or innocent Jennifer Ballard appeared, she was not to be trusted until he was absolutely certain it was safe to do so.

She would have to prove to him beyond a shadow of a doubt that she was telling the truth.

BY TWELVE-THIRTY Ethan parked in front of the office at the Blue Moon Motel on the outskirts of Kankakee. It was a quaint joint to say the least. It reminded him of the kind of place hookers took their johns. If the esteemed Dr. Ballard had been looking for a low profile, she'd found it in a big way.

Ethan emerged cautiously from his vehicle. As he repositioned the gun at the small of his back, he surveyed the empty parking area as well as the row of vacant-looking, rundown rooms on either side of the office. The sign proclaiming Vacancies hung at an odd angle near the door. Faded blue paint was cracked and peeling from the antiquated wood siding. It was a real dump.

Still scanning warily, Ethan walked up the steps and across the small porch that led to the office. The July humidity was sweltering. Inside, the office proved no cooler. A small oscillating fan kept the fetid air moving, but did nothing to cool the temperature.

A short, bald man with a cigarette dangling from one corner of his mouth dragged his attention from the soap opera he was watching on the small television set. "Can I help you?" he asked with absolute disinterest. He didn't even bother to rise from his dilapidated chair.

Ethan narrowed his gaze and set his lips in a grim line, a practiced move that boasted of the impatience radiating behind the expression and should serve to motivate the listless clerk. ''I certainly hope so.''

The guy appeared startled then. He shot to his feet. It was almost as if he'd looked at Ethan for the first time and noted what could only be called trouble. Ethan knew he presented a somewhat dangerous persona, and that was fine by him, especially at times like this. It allowed for a certain ease in getting what he wanted. He could well imagine what the guy behind the scarred counter thought at the moment. Ethan's shoulder-length hair was tied back in a queue. A small silver hoop embellished one ear. But it was his size more than anything else that served as the most persuasive. He was six-four and weighed a muscular 220 pounds. Not too many people willingly messed with him. And that's the way he liked it.

If the now-flustered clerk didn't stop gaping Ethan was pretty sure the lit cancer stick was going to fall right out of his mouth.

''I need a room. My name is Ethan Delaney. I hope I don't need a reservation.'' He said the last a bit facetiously.

Clenching his lips together to grip the cigarette, the guy shook his head, then abruptly changed it to a nod. ''You…you already have a room,'' he stammered. He grabbed a key. ''One fourteen.'' He angled his head to his left. ''All the way at the end.''

Ethan wasn't surprised. Dr. Jennifer Ballard, if that was who she really was, was supposed to be waiting for him. She certainly wouldn't risk using her real name if she was in hiding. He supposed that was the reason she'd used his.

"Thank you," he said as he reached for the key.

The man behind the counter swallowed hard as he dropped the key into Ethan's hand. "Just...just let me know if you need anything else."

"Just one thing," Ethan said pointedly.

The guy jumped. "Yeah?"

Ethan dropped a couple of bills on the counter. "I haven't been here, got it?"

The clerk's head bobbed up and down as he pocketed the money. "Never saw you."

Ethan smiled, something several degrees shy of pleasant. "Good."

As the clerk said, room 114 was all the way at the end. The six rooms before it appeared empty, just as Ethan had suspected when he arrived. He had no doubt that the seven rooms on the other side of the office were just as empty. Glancing from right to left once more, he reached for his gun and simultaneously shoved the key into the lock. He pushed open the door.

To his surprise it was dark inside, but blessedly cool. The drapes were pulled tight. He felt for the light switch but a distinctly feminine voice stopped him.

"Close the door first."

Moving into defensive mode, Ethan closed the door behind him and tightened his fingers on the weapon.

"Now you can turn on the light."

He flipped the switch, blinked once to focus, his gun leveled in the direction of the sound of her voice.

A woman who looked no older than seventeen or

eighteen, clad in tattered hip-hugger jeans and a cut-off T-shirt stood on the opposite side of the room. She wasn't very tall, five-two maybe, and waif-thin. Long blond hair, pale blue eyes, elfin features. Ethan couldn't say for sure if she was Dr. Jennifer Ballard or not, but she definitely resembled the girl in the five-year-old photograph he'd seen. With one major exception—this woman was holding on tight with both hands to a small-caliber handgun, the barrel pointed at his chest.

"I need to see some identification, Mr. Delaney." She moistened her lips and exhaled a shaky breath. "But first, I'll need you to put your gun down."

# Chapter Two

*Please, God,* Jenn Ballard prayed, *don't let him realize this gun isn't loaded.*

"I said, put your gun down," she repeated to the large, dangerous-looking man standing on the other side of a bed that would prove less than adequate as a protective barrier.

"I don't think so," he said quietly. "Why don't you put yours away and then I'll do the same."

She trembled at the sound of his voice. Smooth but lethal. What should she do? She'd expected him to obey her command. They always did in the movies…the ones she watched anyway.

She had no other choice. Gritting her teeth for courage, she drew the hammer back, cocking the weapon just as she'd seen guys like Clint Eastwood do. The resounding click echoed loudly in the still room. "Put it down *now,*" she demanded with as much gravity as she could marshal. She sure hoped all those late-night movies she used to watch weren't wrong.

The man, whom she prayed was really Ethan Delaney, stared at her for two endless seconds before he relented. She let go the breath she'd been holding when he placed his weapon on the bedspread. Thank God.

"Now, the ID," she reminded.

"Just stay cool, lady." He opened the left lapel of his lightweight leather jacket wide, showing her he had nothing to hide, and reached with his thumb and forefinger into an interior pocket. His evaluating stare never left her as he produced a small black leather credentials case. He tossed it onto the bed still eyeing her speculatively. She knew how she looked, but she couldn't help that. The ragged jeans and the midriff top were the best she could do under the circumstances. The fact that the getup was reasonably clean had been her only concern when she'd bartered for it. With her hair down instead of in its usual neat bun and sporting the funky clothes she doubted anyone would recognize her. Even her beloved fiancé.

Which was the whole point.

Never taking her eyes off the man looming a mere mattress width away, she reached for the case he'd tossed onto the bed. She flipped it open and glanced at the Colby Agency picture ID. Ethan Delaney. Thirty-four, six-four, 220 pounds. Brown hair and eyes. She looked back and forth between the ID and the man himself. The hair was really long, tied back in a ponytail, and the eyes an uncommonly dark coppery brown. Her throat went a little dry. A guy this size could definitely do some damage. Maybe she shouldn't have begun their meeting in such an unfriendly, distrustful manner.

"Satisfied?" he asked pointedly.

Oh, yes. She'd definitely made a mistake. But what choice had she had?

None.

She nodded, then lowered her weapon. "Sorry about that, but you can't imagine how frightened I've been." Suddenly feeling too weary, she dropped both her gun and the ID case onto the bed. "I'm glad you're here."

He reached for his gun, tucked it into the waistband of his jeans, and snagged hers up next along with his ID. Once the ID was back in his pocket he checked her weapon.

The glare that followed was penetrating, fierce. "Did you know this weapon isn't loaded?"

She collapsed onto the edge of the bed. She was too exhausted and too emotionally wiped out to explain fully. "Yes," she admitted. "I didn't have anything left to trade for bullets."

That piercing gaze intensified. "Trade? What the hell are you talking about?"

She shrugged tiredly. "I had to make a run for it with no money or plastic. I met a guy in an alley near the bus station who traded me the gun for my Rolex. I'd already traded my engagement ring for a bus ticket out of Chicago and my shoes for these clothes and sneakers. I didn't have anything left."

"You are kidding, right?"

Indignant, she shook her head. "I didn't have any choice." What was the big deal? Though she couldn't accurately assess the value of the engagement ring, it could have been as fake as her fiancé. The remainder of the items had been top of the line. The girl who got her shoes certainly got the better bargain. They were Guccis after all. The wedding dress a Vera Wang, but it had been ruined, and she'd had to cram it into a trash bin. The horrible memories she'd kept at bay for nearly 72 hours now spilled one over the other into her weary mind.

Her stomach roiled. There had been so much blood. Uncle Russ was dead.

She blinked back the tears that threatened. She had to be strong, had to get back to her father. His already fragile life might be in danger, too. No matter what else happened, she had to have help getting her life back. She had to make sure *he* didn't hurt her father. Her father's safety was of primary importance. With his health so poor, almost anything could finish him off. She couldn't bear the thought of losing him yet, and certainly not like this.

The man, Ethan Delaney, looked at her with something new in his eyes…pity, maybe? Anger kindled in her belly and was joined by indignation. She didn't need his pity; she needed his investigative expertise.

"When did you eat last?" he asked quietly, concerned.

She thought about that one for a moment, then remembered. The last three days were like one big blur of runaway emotions in her memory, some images more vivid than others. She immediately pushed those away. "The man at the front desk gave me a bag of peanuts and a soft drink when I checked in this morning," she admitted. "Since I didn't have any money I was profoundly grateful."

"Really?" Ethan said, clearly skeptical. He lifted an eyebrow in punctuation. "How'd you pay when you checked in if you didn't have any money or plastic?"

He probably wasn't going to like this part. "I told him the man I was expecting would pay. Apparently that's customary at this establishment."

Ethan puffed out an impatient breath, then massaged his chin trying to decide what to do with her. Finally, as if he'd fought his own better judgment and lost, he shook his head. "Let's go get you something to eat, then we'll talk."

She swung her head side to side in adamant disagreement of his suggestion. "I don't feel leaving the room would be a wise move until we come to an agreement. Can't you call for something to be delivered?"

His facial features set in grim lines, he stalked over to the table next to the bed and jerked the single drawer open. She tried not to dwell on the fact that she'd already alienated her only hope and they'd barely met. She had to work seriously on her people skills. But first, before anything else, she had to convince him to believe her. Success depended solely on that one step.

After checking the yellow pages, he asked, "Pizza okay?"

Her stomach clenched in anticipation. "Yes." It wasn't the cuisine she usually preferred, but it would certainly do. She was starved.

After he'd placed the order, he sat down in the only chair in the room, his expression unreadable. "The pizza'll be here in twenty minutes." He leveled that dark, analyzing gaze on her once more, making her tremble in spite of her best efforts not to. "I know who your father is and most everything I need to know about the company, BalPhar. But I need you to start at the beginning and tell me why you think someone is trying to kill you."

His apathy infuriated her. "I don't *think*," she said hotly, "I *know*." She glared at him, though she was confident her killer stare was not nearly as effective as his.

He lifted one shoulder and let it fall, the gesture as nonchalant as his tone and all the more infuriating. "Then tell me how you *know*."

She drew in a deep, bolstering breath and started at the beginning as he'd requested, but opted for the abbreviated version. "Five years ago my father began a new research project with another scientist, Dr. Kessler. As the research progressed, Dr. Kessler made extraordinary advances. Then two years ago another scientist came on board with the project. With his help, the results rocketed to a whole new level."

She was so tired. None of what she was about to say could be proven. How could she expect an outsider to accept it? How could it even be happening? Her father had always been so careful. How would she ever make this man believe the unbelievable tale she was about to relay? It was real and she had to have his help. Her father trusted Victoria Colby. If Victoria had sent this guy, Jenn had to trust him. But she couldn't tell him everything—not yet. If she told him too much too fast, he would never believe her. Some things a person had to see with their own eyes.

She rubbed at her temples and stretched her neck in a bid for more time, then went on, ''About a year ago there was a falling out between the two lead scientists and Dr. Kessler left. Now, the project named after him is ready to move to the next level—testing on human subjects.''

''Kessler is out of the picture completely?'' Delaney wanted to know.

She nodded. ''He won't have anything to do with BalPhar. He even refuses his share of the stocks.''

That revelation made headway with her so-far unimpressable guest. He looked somewhat more interested.

He asked no questions, so she continued. ''The drug created is a chemotherapy agent that literally neutralizes cancer cells. It's called Cellneu.''

She noted another almost imperceptible change in those dark eyes. Even she felt amazed at how the drug worked. ''Astonishing, isn't it?''

''And very valuable,'' he suggested.

''Very.'' That one drug would make BalPhar a fortune a dozen times over and has the potential of saving countless lives. ''There's only one problem,'' she added, but hesitated before going on. She had absolutely no proof of what she was about to say.

He studied her for a moment, considering what she'd told him so far. ''Is that why you think someone is trying to kill you? To steal your new drug?''

She shook her head. ''Someone *is* trying to kill me,'' she explained, ''because I know something he doesn't want me to.''

Delaney gestured with his hand for her to continue. "Don't keep me in suspense."

Jenn moistened her lips. She knew how this was going to sound. She could only hope that he would believe her. "There's something wrong with the drug. It may be dangerous to humans in the long run. I think maybe that's why Kessler got out."

"Can you prove it?"

She sighed. There was the one sticking point. She stood then, hands on hips for emphasis. She had no evidence, just the word of a dying man. "I can't prove it, but I know it's true."

"And how do you know this?" he asked calmly. So damned calmly she wanted to scream.

"Because my uncle, who worked on the project, whom I trusted implicitly, told me with his dying breath."

One of those dark eyebrows quirked. "His dying breath?"

"My fiancé killed him. He would have killed me, too, but I got away."

Delaney leaned forward, bracing his forearms on his widespread knees. "Where exactly did this take place? Were there any witnesses?"

"In the chapel where I was about to be married." She tried to blink away the images again, but couldn't stop them. Her blood-stained gown. Russ lying lifeless on the floor. The sinister look in David's eyes. Jenn pressed her fingertips to her closed lids and tried to banish the ugly pictures her mind conjured. Russ was dead. Was her father dead already, too? "There weren't any witnesses. We wanted to keep things quiet. The others present worked for my fiancé. Even the minister.'' She remembered vividly his doing nothing to help her as the man dragged her away. The minister simply stared at her, a passive expression on his face.

Delaney stood and started in her direction. Startled, Jenn tensed. In a protective move, she wrapped her arms around her middle. *Be strong.*

He towered over her. Intimidating, commanding. A little hitch disrupted her breathing as her senses absorbed his nearness. His scent. The heat he radiated. The restrained power behind all that muscle. She fought the fear. He was supposed to be on her side. *No fear.*

''So you were at this chapel, garbed in full wedding attire,'' he clarified as emotionlessly as if he were inquiring about the time of day, ''ready to walk down the aisle and your fiancé tried to kill you. *But you got away.* Is that what you're saying?''

He didn't believe her. Fury swept through Jenn, evaporating the last of her fear. She had no reason to lie. Couldn't he understand that? ''Basically, yes,'' she returned tightly. ''Except that he ordered one of his men to kill me. He dragged me from the chapel, then drove deep into the woods.'' She shivered, knowing for the first time in her life how Snow White had felt. ''He made me watch while he dug a shallow grave. When he decided to have himself a little fun before he killed me, I managed to get a grip on the shovel. I hit him hard, then ran as fast as I could.'' She shuddered. ''I didn't look back.''

''All right.'' Delaney still looked ambivalent. ''Why

don't you give me your fiancé's name and I'll call a detective friend of mine in the city and have him pick the guy up. It shouldn't take us long to sort this out.''

Fear rocketed through her. ''We can't call the police!''

Delaney inclined his head, studying her from another angle. ''Why not? You said he murdered your uncle and that he attempted to have you killed.''

She chewed her lower lip. She couldn't let him call the police. ''He…he has my father. If I call the police and they investigate, but don't lock him up, I know he'll kill my father.'' Panic tightened her chest. Though her father was gravely ill, on the verge of death really, she didn't want him suffering. ''Please.'' She advanced on Ethan Delaney and grabbed him by his jacket. ''Please don't risk making things worse for my father. You have to help me.''

Those dark eyes softened just a fraction. ''Tell me the name of this fiancé that you're so afraid of and I'll see what I can do.''

She nodded and swiped at the tears welling. ''His name is David Crane. Dr. David Crane.''

TWO AND ONE HALF hours later and Ethan was sitting in the reception area outside Dr. David Crane's plush tenth-story office at Ballard Pharmaceuticals.

It had taken Ethan a full half hour to convince his client to go along with his plan. She'd done everything short of crying to dissuade him, and she'd been damn close to doing that. Once he'd explained exactly what he intended to do, she'd reluctantly gone along with him. He'd asked her a few more questions about the Kessler Project as she wolfed down half the pizza he'd ordered. Though he was still skeptical of just who she was, he recognized that she was extremely intelligent and appeared to know almost everything about the company.

Her resourcefulness surprised him. He'd expected a spoiled rich kid who couldn't fend for herself outside a closely structured environment. If all she said was true, she'd outwitted a would-be killer, run for her life, found a way to disguise herself and gotten the hell out of Dodge all on her own.

Impressive, he had to admit.

But, damn, she looked so young. Especially dressed as she was. He gritted his teeth and forced away the things he shouldn't think about…like that smart and too sexy mouth of hers. Her lips had a daring little pucker to them…one that begged to be kissed, even if it was clearly unintentional. She was small, but emanated an air of strength. She'd sure surprised the hell out of him. In more ways than one.

On a more professional note, if she wasn't Jennifer Ballard, she was certainly someone high up at BalPhar or a well-trained spy for one of their competitors. In his estimation, she knew far too much not to be from the inside. And if she wasn't Jennifer, where was the real Jennifer Ballard?

Necessity had never posed the occasion for him to visit Ballard Pharmaceuticals before. He was impressed with the place. The building sat in the middle of a large compound, fifteen or twenty acres at least, a good twenty miles from any real civilization to speak of. Security was top-notch. Ten floors and a basement defined the structure. The architecture presented a very futuristic feel with sleek lines and angles, but with an underlying cold, stainless-steel edge.

If Jennifer Ballard had grown up in this cool, seemingly untouchable environment he wondered how she had developed any emotions at all. The austere feel of the place didn't sit well with him. But he was still collecting data, physically and mentally. He wouldn't make any judgments just yet.

"Mr. Delaney," the well-polished, efficient-looking secretary said, her voice a perfectly modulated pitch, "Dr. Crane will see you now."

Ethan wondered if she'd taken voice lessons to achieve that flawless inflection. "Thank you." He stood and nodded once in her direction, then turned toward the door a few feet away that opened into the junior VP's office. He wondered then if Crane would remember him. He almost laughed. Ethan supposed he would. It was difficult to forget the man who'd saved one's life. He should know, Crane had saved his as well. The three days and nights they'd spent together making their way across that desert were permanently imprinted upon his brain. No way he could ever forget. Death had stalked them both in more than one form. Ultimately, they'd saved each other.

Crane was standing when Ethan entered his office. "Ethan, what an honor to have you here. To what do I owe this pleasure?" He clasped Ethan's hand and shook it heartily the moment Ethan had extended it. "How long has it been?"

"Too long." Ethan smiled. Crane had done well for himself. He still looked fit and had aged well. Lots of men in his line of work would have grown soft and maybe even gained a spare tire. But not Crane. He looked in excellent physical condition, seemed very much in charge. "It's good to see you, too, Dr. Crane," Ethan said after his quick visual assessment.

Crane waved him off. "Don't be ridiculous. Call me David. After what we've been through together, formalities are a slap in the face. Have a seat. Please."

Ethan sat down in one of the lavish leather chairs facing Crane's desk. "Looks like you've moved up in the world," he commented as he glanced around the luxurious office. A wall of windows presented a picturesque view near the long conference table on the other side of the room. From this level, everything for miles around sprawled across the landscape in a sea of lush green forests interrupted only by a narrow, curving road that led back to the city. The office furnishings were ornate, the decorating classic. It was nothing like the rest of what Ethan had seen in the building.

"From a desert in Iraq," Crane nodded "I've definitely moved up." He leaned back in his chair. "I have to say, I like it a lot better here."

Ethan laughed. "I'll bet you do." An expensive-looking abstract oil painting hung on the wall behind Crane's desk. The colors were so vivid it almost looked three-dimensional. The artwork nagged at Ethan, but he couldn't quite put his finger on precisely what it was that bothered him.

"May I get you something to drink?" Crane offered, gesturing to the tray on the massive mahogany sideboard near the conference table.

Ethan dragged his attention back to the man and said, "No. I'm good."

Crane propped his elbows on the chair arms and steepled his fingers. "My secretary tells me you're with the Colby Agency now. BalPhar has done business with Victoria Colby for years. Sounds as if you haven't done so badly yourself."

"It's not that different from what I used to do," Ethan allowed, and that was true to an extent.

Crane nodded. "I can imagine." He frowned then. "You know, I have a meeting in a few minutes that I, unfortunately, can't reschedule, I think we should have dinner this evening and talk about old times," he suggested, his frown reverting to a smile. "You can tell me what you've been up to since you saved my life all those years ago."

Ethan searched Crane's expression and posture for any sign of deception, but found none. "I wouldn't have been able to get you out of that desert if you hadn't saved my life first."

"I suppose that's true," Crane admitted with a nonchalant lift of one shoulder. "But I would never have gotten out of there, period, without you. I was a dead man." He pressed Ethan with a fiercely sincere gaze. "You saved my life. I owe you for that." He smiled again, pushing aside the intensity he'd just displayed. "So tell me what I can do for you. Anything. Name it."

Crane looked straight at Ethan, his gaze open, honest. The man Ethan had known all those years ago would not have been able to conceal lies so well. Surely he had not become a master of deception in the intervening time. Jennifer Ballard had to be wrong. Or maybe this was some sort of setup. There was no way to tell yet who was setting up whom.

"I'm investigating a small research facility for one of your competitors," Ethan explained, laying out the cover he'd assured his client would prevent any questions as to why he was at BalPhar. "Alexon wants to buy out Camden, but they're not certain it's a wise investment. I'm sure you're familiar with Camden." He paused for effect. "Do you know anything that might make a difference as to whether Alexon proceeds? I know I'm taking a risk letting you in on what Alexon has planned, but I felt I could trust you."

Crane pressed his chin to his steepled fingers and considered the question as well as Ethan's final profound statement. "We've worked with Camden from time to time and never had any problem. Their reputation is solid, but financially they're on the rocks." A frown furrowed Crane's brow. "However, financial woes aside, I didn't know they were for sale. I am surprised at that. Howard Camden always swore he'd never answer to anyone else."

Ethan smiled. "Camden doesn't know it just yet."

"Ah-ha." Crane nodded knowingly. "A hostile take-over. Interesting."

"Alexon wants the heads-up on a new cancer drug Camden's got in the works." Ethan shrugged, feigning disinterest. "You'd know more about that kind of thing than me. It's some sort of cell-neutralizing agent related to cancer treatment. Big money-maker, I'm told, for the company that comes out with it first."

Crane stilled, but showed no other outward indication of uneasiness or suspicion. "Really? I hadn't heard about that either. Do you know if they're ready to go public?"

There was the ever-so-slightest hint of wariness in Crane's last question. Ethan had struck a nerve. Ethan flared his hands in feigned innocence. "Nah, that's all I was told." He narrowed his gaze on Crane. "So, you think Camden's a good investment?"

There was something different in Crane's eyes now. Ethan considered vaguely that maybe Crane was calculating how he could buy Camden first. Too bad it wasn't really for sale. And Camden definitely didn't have the cell-neutralizing drug in the works. The head of security at Alexon, an old friend of Victoria's, had suggested this fishing expedition. One quick phone call was all it had taken. Next to BalPhar, Alexon was the biggest pharmaceuticals corporation in the country. Ethan had been right to mention the new drug, the one from the Kessler Project. He definitely had captured Crane's attention—or suspicion—now.

"If Camden is on the verge of some sort of major breakthrough, it would definitely be a wise investment," Crane advised. "However, you have to consider that many times rumors are started to make a business look attractive when it really isn't,'' he said, his tone direct. ''If Camden actually were on the precipice of something that big, I doubt there would be any rumors. There would be tight control. Very tight control,'' he emphasized. ''You might want to reevaluate your sources.''

''I hadn't thought of that,'' Ethan lied. ''I suppose if Camden is having financial woes, this sort of rumor could definitely be to their benefit.''

''Absolutely.''

Ethan stood. Crane did the same. Oddly he offered no objection to Ethan's leaving, nor did he bring up dinner again.

''Thanks for your input.'' Ethan extended his hand once more. ''Maybe I can do the same for you some-time.''

Crane shook his hand. ''The Colby Agency already takes very good care of us, but I'll keep that in mind.''

Ethan hesitated before he turned to leave. ''By the way, Victoria asked me to inquire about Mr. Ballard's health.''

Crane's expression grew somber. ''Not well, I'm afraid. He's rarely lucid these days.''

''I'm sorry to hear that,'' Ethan said. ''And his daughter, Jennifer, how is she, under the circum-stances?''

''She's holding up as well as can be expected,'' Crane responded without hesitation.

''Perhaps I should stop in, offer the agency's sup-port.''

"She's in Boston on business," Crane said quickly, too quickly. "I'll tell her that Mrs. Colby asked."

Ethan nodded. "You do that."

Ethan left the office. He took his time strolling to the elevator. Though he still wasn't sure Crane was hiding anything earth-shaking and certainly didn't believe him to be the monster Jennifer Ballard had drawn, Ethan had the distinct impression that he was being watched as he made his exit.

DAVID CRANE stood silently at his desk for several moments after Delaney left. David watched him leave the building on the private monitor that was usually disguised as a rather expensive oil painting. He had a very bad feeling about his old friend's visit. David clenched his jaw to hold back the fury whipping through him.

Someone knew. But no one—*absolutely no one*— was supposed to know. Only one of two people could have set this afternoon's events into motion. Kessler possibly, but David doubted it, though he would certainly have one of his men look into that prospect. Kessler hadn't opened his mouth in all this time, why would he do so now? He knew the consequences if he did. Kessler enjoyed his family...enjoyed life. He knew enough about this business to know that running his mouth off would get him killed. David would have killed him months ago, but that would only have aroused suspicions.

Kessler knew better than to talk. And if it wasn't Kessler, then it could only be one other person.

But she was supposed to be dead.

David pressed the intercom button for his chief of security. "I want Ethan Delaney followed. I want to know where he goes and with whom he speaks."

"Yes, sir, Dr. Crane."

David sank back into his chair, a muscle flexing rhythmically in his tense jaw. Delaney couldn't know anything…not really.

Because *she* was dead.

He was sure of it.

He'd ordered the contract personally.

# Chapter Three

The moment Ethan Delaney had walked out of the tiny motel room, Jenn had started to pace. Nearly three hours later she had worked herself into a ball of nerves.

What was taking him so long?

She should never have allowed him to talk her into going along with this crazy idea. What had possessed her? She tunneled her fingers through her hair and huffed with exasperation. It was a mistake. She knew David too well. He would smooth-talk and manipulate until he uncovered the truth.

And then he would come after her.

Fear surged through her veins.

She should just get out of here now while she still could.

Jenn stalled in the middle of the room. She twisted her hands together and fought for composure. Where could she go? She had no money and nothing of real value left to trade.

Well, nothing except her body. She cringed. The motel clerk's rude suggestions echoed inside her head. He'd offered to give her the room for free if she'd...

Jenn shuddered. She didn't want to think about that. She would figure out a way to do whatever she had to without resorting to such desperate measures. If she could only go to the police. She sighed wearily. But she couldn't. There were too many questions she couldn't answer. David had set her up thoroughly. She had no way to prove who she was...no way to prove anything. And worst of all, no one even knew she was missing. Except a private investigator who really didn't believe her.

She sank down onto the end of the bed. She'd been so stupid. How could she not have seen who David really was? She couldn't say that she'd been head over heels in love with him or blinded by passion, but she had cared deeply for him, trusted him completely. She'd felt safe with David. Especially after her father had grown so ill. Lord knew he was fading fast. With no other family except her Uncle Russ who was even older than her father, David was all she would have when those two were gone. David and the children they planned to have together. What a fool she'd been.

Jenn dropped her head into her hands and cried for the first time since she'd watched her uncle die in her arms. Her chest ached with worry for her father. She might never see him again, never have the opportunity to say goodbye. She had to find a way to get back home before it was too late.

But David had stolen her life. She didn't know how he'd managed it. She scrubbed the dampness from her face and shook her head. It was so...surreal. No one would ever believe her. And, to be honest, she found it hard to believe herself. How would she ever prove she was Jennifer Ballard? The only place her fingerprints or DNA were on file was at BalPhar. In all likelihood, David had already taken care of that. He was far too smart to allow such a simple mistake to ruin his master plan. Hadn't she seen proof of that already? Her dentist's office burning to the ground could not have been a coincidence. David had known that was the only other identifying source available to her outside the walls of BalPhar.

Ultimately it was her own fault that she didn't have any other recourse. She had forgone a social life for as long as she could remember. She'd spent her entire existence either in school concentrating on her education, or in the lab with her father helping to develop some new drug or anti-viral serum. She had no friends, no one who could help her in any way.

Determined not to be undone by the likes of David Crane, she pushed to her feet, her frustration fueling her bravado. Well, she wasn't about to sit around here feeling sorry for herself or waiting for David to send his henchmen to finish what they'd started.

She was out of here.

Reclaiming her unloaded gun that Delaney had left on the bedside table, she tucked it into the back of her waistband the same way she'd seen him do. It might be unloaded, but it was hers. There was always the possibility she could trade it for something of value. A bus ticket…or meal, she thought, striving for optimism. See, she mused, she wasn't as bad off as she'd thought.

Squaring her shoulders, she headed for the door. The

sound of a key turning in the lock stopped her dead in her tracks. She watched the knob turn and the door swing inward. She stumbled back. Oh God! Had David found her? Delaney should have been back long ago. What if they'd joined forces against her?

Her heart stopped completely during the endless second it took her brain to assimilate what her eyes saw.

*Delaney.*

He stepped into the room, closing the door behind him. The size of the room diminished instantly around his towering frame.

"You're back," Jenn murmured the obvious and with a relief she couldn't quite conceal.

He cocked an eyebrow. "Was there any question?"

She shook her head. "No. No. You'd been gone for a while and I was beginning to get a little concerned. That's all."

A little? Now there was the understatement of the century. She'd freaked out completely. And she never freaked out. Just another thing David had stolen from her...her self-confidence.

Delaney's evaluating gaze lingered on her for far too long before he took another look around the room. "You weren't planning on splitting on me now, were you?"

She blinked to shield the lie in her eyes, then moistened her incredibly dry lips. "Of course not. I was just anxious that's all." Her hands fluttered in the air as if she might be able to grasp an appropriate response there. No such luck. "I was pacing. You know, anxious."

That dark gaze scanned the room for about three more seconds, then lit on hers once more. His suspicion was crystal clear. He'd noted the gun missing from where he'd left it on the bedside table. "Where's the gun?"

Irritation lined her brow. "The what?"

"The gun," he said, fury snapping in his brown eyes. "Where's the handgun you traded your Rolex for?"

Instinctively, she backed up a step. "I...I don't know. I thought you had it." The bathroom. If she could make it to the bathroom, she could put the gun on the toilet tank and pretend it had been there the whole time. Then he'd never know she'd planned to make a run for it.

Before she could make a move in that direction his arm snaked around her waist and he had the gun in his hand. "I don't like games, Miss Ballard," he growled. "If I'm going to help you I have to be able to trust you."

She couldn't think...she couldn't speak. He'd stolen her breath as easily as he'd taken the gun. His arm felt like a steel band, his massive chest like unyielding stone beneath her palms. That chiseled face was only inches from hers, a fierce scowl marring the undeniably interesting lines and angles there.

"Let me go," she demanded the instant she found her voice. The command was a little shaky, but clear nonetheless. "And that's *Dr. Ballard,*" she added when he failed to immediately release her. He wasn't the only one who could intimidate. She might not have the physical strength, but she had other assets...like superior intelligence. She glared at him, hoping he could read her mind.

His arm fell away.

She scrambled back from his reach.

"Sit," he ordered and inclined his head toward the bed.

The heart that had all but stilled in her chest a few moments ago now pounded erratically. She looked at the bed and then at him. What did he have in mind? A new kind of fear rushed through her. Surely a reputable agency like Victoria Colby's wouldn't allow their investigators to—

He exhaled an audibly frustrated breath derailing her thought. "Don't worry, I'm not into frightened little girls. We need to talk. *Just talk.* Now sit," he repeated, leaning nearer, ratcheting up the intimidation level.

Still reeling with the fight-or-flight impulse, she plopped down on the very edge of the bed. She hated this he-man, macho crap, but she didn't have enough bravado left in her to put up a fuss about his calling her a frightened little girl. She'd show him. She was the paying customer after all. He was supposed to follow *her* orders. Furious, she braced her hands on either side of her, just in case she got another chance to make a run for it. If he'd told David she was here, she was dead. That was the bottom line.

"I met with Crane," Delaney said, his voice neutral as he settled into the chair. He had no intention of giving anything away with his tone or his facial expressions. That much was evident.

"What did you find out?" She couldn't keep the anxiety out of her voice despite the irritation she felt at his secretiveness. David Crane was the man who'd ordered her execution. She had a right to know everything.

Dear God, if he suspected...

"What did he say?" she demanded when Delaney didn't respond quickly enough to suit her.

"He was calm and collected." Delaney looked directly at her, watching, analyzing. "He never mentioned there was a problem or that you were even missing."

Her throat constricted as fear rocketed to the forefront. "He didn't suspect why you were really there? You're sure about that?"

"I'm positive."

Jenn breathed her first sigh of relief in more than three days. "Thank God."

"When I asked about you, he said you were in Boston on business."

Ire pricked her. "Well, obviously he was lying."

"Obviously," Delaney parroted dryly.

"What is that supposed to mean?" Her fingers fisted in the faded floral bedspread. For the first time in her life she actually felt the overwhelming desire to hit something—or someone, to be specific.

"Look." Delaney leaned forward, bracing his forearms on his knees. "We've got a problem here. You refuse to go to the police. That puts me in an awkward position since you can't prove you're who you say you are, and nothing appears to be amiss at your company—"

"Nothing amiss?" she echoed, surging to her feet. "How do I get this through that thick skull of yours?

He thinks I'm dead. He ordered one of his cronies to execute me. I'm confident that he has every intention of hunting me down and finishing the job. I've only gotten by so far on borrowed time. *He wants me dead.*" She flung her arms wide. "What do I have to say? What do you want from me?"

"All I'm saying," Delaney said calmly, "is that we need proof. You're going to have to give me something more than this unverifiable story. Your uncle's body hasn't shown up, at least it hasn't been reported in the media. There's absolutely no evidence that anything has happened. If you're afraid to confront Crane face-to-face, then we need evidence."

"And how am I supposed to get that?" She started pacing again. This was insane. Unless she could get into the lab and find fingerprint or DNA sequencing that he hadn't tampered with already, she was screwed. Delaney just didn't know how badly yet. A face-to-face confrontation was out of the question. "I don't have any ID," she ranted. "I can't go to the police. And David is covering for my absence in more ways than you know. The only proof that might exist is at BalPhar." Could she tell him the rest now? Would he call the men in the little white suits if she dared?

He stood, disrupting the calm she'd managed to begin to recover. She tried to look strong, but probably didn't.

"I'd like you to come back to Chicago with me. There's someone I want you to see."

This was bad. She had that feeling. The hair prickled on the back of her neck. Something heavy, pepperoni probably, settled in the pit of her stomach. That feeling that always warned her—had never failed her. Except once. Trusting David Crane had been the biggest mistake of her life and she'd had no warning at all.

Slowly she inched a step closer to the door. "I don't know if going back to Chicago would be such a good idea." Though technically BalPhar was north of Aurora, Chicago was too close for comfort right now. She had to have the Colby Agency firmly on her side first.

He recovered that same inch or two she'd lengthened between them. "I won't let anything happen to you. You have my word."

She knew a moment's pause. Maybe he was telling the truth. Maybe he really did want to help her. She had to start somewhere and her father trusted Victoria Colby. But how could she trust anyone ever again? Especially a man!

"Who is it you'd like me to see?"

The hesitation before he responded answered the next question before she even asked it.

"His name is Clarence Melbourne. Dr. Clarence Melbourne. The agency uses him from time to time."

Fury ignited inside her. "What kind of doctor?" she demanded but she already knew. He'd told her without even mentioning a specialty.

"He's a psychologist. I'd like him to do a quick evaluation just to be sure."

She moved another step toward the door. "Just to be sure of what?"

He was closer now. Had he moved again without her noticing? She couldn't be sure. She'd thought she'd managed to increase the distance between them, but somehow she hadn't. Somehow he was closer.

"Think, Jennifer," he said quietly, using her first name in an attempt to bring the discussion down to a more personal level. She knew exactly what he was doing. "We both want the same thing, to solve your problem. Your father would never have used the Colby Agency without checking us out first. I just need to be sure of you. Can you understand that? Just a few questions and a few minutes of your time. That's all it will take. There's nothing to be concerned about."

The sincerity in those dark eyes *almost* convinced her.

"Can you do that for me?" he asked, the words barely more than a whisper.

Her fingers clenched around the doorknob behind her back. "I...I don't know," she stammered, buying time. "I thought we were supposed to be doing this my way. After all, I'm the customer. Isn't the customer always right?" She prayed his voice when he responded would conceal the sound of the doorknob turning.

"You have to trust me, Jennifer. I won't let anyone hurt you."

How could he sound so genuinely interested in her well-being? For one long beat their gazes held in a kind of wary dance. He'd made up his mind, just as she had.

He lunged at her.

She jerked the door open and flung herself across the threshold.

He yelled for her to wait...not to go outside. She ignored him. And ran like hell.

Which direction? her mind screamed. Right? No! Left. She ran harder. She could hear him right behind her. The gravel under her feet slipped and slid, making it difficult for her to gain purchase. She had to run faster.

Faster!

His arms went around her from behind.

She struggled, twisting around and kicking for all she was worth.

"Dammit! Stop fighting me," he growled. "I have to get you back inside."

"Let me go!" She pounded his chest. Grabbed at his hair. Still he wouldn't let go.

Her heart pounded like a drum. She had to get away. He was going to take her back to Chicago. She couldn't go back to Chicago. She kicked frantically as he carried her back toward the room. Her sneaker made contact with a shin. Another savage growl rumbled from the chest he had her plastered against.

Once he had her inside the room, he closed and locked the door then tossed her onto the bed. "Don't move," he warned, his tone deadly, his expression barbaric.

He glared at her. She tried to control her breathing, the ragged sound splintering the silence. Calm down, she told herself. But she couldn't. Tears burned her eyes, but she fought them back. She would not cry. *She would not cry!*

She scrambled up onto all fours in the middle of the bed and glared back at the man standing between her and freedom. "You can't make me go anywhere. I will find a way to get away from you. Besides,'' she huffed, "it's a free country.''

Something in his eyes changed. The metamorphosis was chilling. Ice glazed the surface of those dark coppery depths, glistening with danger. "I wouldn't get my hopes up, little girl, if I were you.''

Her lips trembled. Ethan wanted to curse himself, long, loud and profusely, for allowing the situation to escalate almost beyond his control. Professionalism had gone out the window the moment he laid eyes on her. He should have stopped her before she made it to the door, much less outside. Whoever had followed him had no doubt seen her if they were still out there.

And he was pretty damned sure they were.

He still had no reason to believe Crane'd had him followed, but *someone* from BalPhar definitely had.

She was poised on her hands and knees in the middle of the bed, ready to run like hell the first chance she got. All that silky blond hair cascaded down her slender arms, making her look at once wild and untamable and frightened and innocent. He took a slow deep breath and counted to ten before he let it out. The instant tightening of male muscle that occurred when his gaze roamed her body made him want to kick his own ass. But it was looking at hers, encased in that snug denim, that was playing havoc with his objectivity. It would help if she didn't look exactly like a sleek, sexy cat ready to pounce on the closest mouse.

He shook himself. What the hell was he thinking? She was a client and far too young for an emotionally burned-out guy like him to be ogling.

"Just stay put and we'll work this out," he placated. Careful not to take his eyes from her wary ones, he backed toward the window. "Just stay cool and we'll talk about it, okay?"

She relaxed marginally. He saw the slightest softening of her rigid posture, but she said nothing. He was relatively certain that wasn't a good sign.

Ethan parted the sixties-style drapes just a fraction and scanned the parking area. His SUV was the only vehicle in the lot, but that didn't lessen his uneasiness.

The rustle of carpet behind him jerked him around at the same instant something crashed into the side of his head. The sound of cheap pottery breaking shattered the quiet of the room. His head spun wildly for a full three seconds after the table lamp made contact with the side of his skull. What remained of the lamp base and yellowed lampshade thumped to the floor.

Instinct kicked in before his equilibrium fully returned. He grabbed an arm, jerking her back when she would have run for the door again. "Don't," he said from between clenched teeth, his face mere inches from hers.

Her eyes were wide with equal measures of fear and fire. She was scared to death of him, but at the same time madder than hell. "I'm not going back until I can prove I'm telling the truth." She flung the words at him, her chest rising and falling with her shallow, rapid breaths, her lips quivering.

"We can't just stay here," he stated bluntly as he set her away from him. A crazy mixture of emotions twisted inside him, undoing him as nothing else had before. He wanted to kiss her every bit as much as he wanted to shake her. It was completely unacceptable. Completely insane. "It might not be safe here anymore," he added as soon as his brain caught up with his instincts.

She backed away from him, her narrowed gaze accusing. "Oh, God. They followed you." She shook her head, huge tears turning those pale blue eyes liquid. "You led them right to me. They'll kill me. I have to—"

Guilt welled inside him. "I told you I wouldn't let anything—"

The ping of breaking glass ended the argument. The drapes shifted once, twice. Another ping. A muffled, but all too familiar splat.

Gunfire!

*Damn.*

Ethan flung himself in front of Jennifer, taking her down to the floor with him. His shoulder took the brunt of the fall, then he rolled her onto her back, careful of the broken lamp, so he could shield her with his body.

Six more hissing puffs echoed in the room. Hole after hole appeared in the plaster. The chair took a hit. Shards of glass scattered over the gold shag carpet. An engine roared. Tires squealed.

Silence abruptly reigned.

Ethan released a grateful breath.

They were finished for the moment.

Jennifer was shaking beneath him.

He went up on his hands and knees above her and gave her a quick visual examination. "Are you hit?"

She shuddered with the effort of holding back a sob. "No," she managed. She tried to push up. "I'm all right."

"Don't." He pressed her back against the floor. "I have to make sure it's clear first."

She nodded, though the prospect appeared to frighten her even more. "Be careful," she murmured.

He didn't take the time to analyze what sounded like worry. "Stay down," he told her again as he shifted to a crouch and then to his feet.

She didn't move as he eased toward the door. He leaned just past the edge of the window and checked the parking area again. Nothing. The shooters must have been waiting at the other end of the long row of rooms. The shooting had probably been a drive-by, but he had to be certain they were gone now.

And there was always the possibility that the motel clerk had called the police.

But it wasn't likely. Not at this dump.

He opened the door an inch at a time. When he could slide his body through the gap he slipped out and down, hitting the ground in one swift, rolling motion, the gun leveled in a firing position.

Nothing.

Except the clerk peeking around the jamb of the office door. "What the hell was that all about?" he cried, his voice quavering.

Still scanning warily, Ethan got to his feet. "You don't want to know."

The guy shook his head frantically. "You're right. I don't."

"Hey." Ethan stopped him before he fled back to the safety of his puny oscillating fan and his soaps. The clerk peeked out once more, eyes wide with fear. "Did you see anything?"

He shook his head vigorously. "Didn't see nothing."

Ethan crossed his hands in front of him, allowing the gun to hold a prominent position. "You're sure about that?"

"A dark blue or black car," the clerk blurted. "That's all. I didn't see the license plate."

"Which way did they go?"

He pointed in the direction of the interstate that led back to Chicago and to Aurora. Ethan figured as much. A dark blue sedan had followed him from BalPhar.

"You can prepare a bill for the broken glass and lamp," Ethan told him. He didn't bother to mention the holes in the wall, they blended well with the damage by previous tenants. "We're leaving."

The guy nodded. He looked faint with relief. "Good idea."

Tucking the gun beneath his jacket, Ethan reentered the room. Jennifer was standing at the end of the bed, her arms folded over her slender middle. Anger glittered in her eyes.

Oh, hell. Just what he needed. More grief from her.

"So," she demanded, tapping one foot for emphasis. "Do you believe me now? I'm fairly certain those were *real* bullets."

"As opposed to *pretend* bullets?" he suggested overbearingly.

She made a disparaging sound and stomped her foot. "You know what I mean! Now, do you believe me?"

Despite his best efforts, one corner of his mouth lifted in a reluctant smile. "Let's just say that I'm a lot more open to the possibility."

THE LIMOUSINE'S cellular phone buzzed. David Crane snatched it up. "Crane," he snapped. It was about time he received a report.

"We followed Delaney to a dump in Kankakee."

"And?"

"*She* was there…waiting for him."

The words reverberated inside David. That was not what he'd wanted to hear.

"I trust you'll remedy the situation," he said tersely. He despised incompetence. He hated cowardice even more. The man he'd trusted to do the job right had failed him and then lied to cover his inability to perform. A smile tugged at David's lips. There was nothing to be done about that now since the man was already dead. One less loose end with which to concern himself. However, David would certainly have accomplished the act in a much slower and more fitting manner if he'd known then what he knew now.

"We'll take care of it, sir."

"There are other complications involved now," he pointed out.

"I understand, sir."

David cleared his throat to ensure that he had the full attention of the man on the other end of the line. "I'm sure you understand the consequences of failure."

"I won't fail."

"Excellent." David disconnected.

She had to die *now*.

He gritted his teeth. He wanted her dead.

Every moment she was alive put the whole project at greater risk…put him at greater risk. Though it disturbed him somewhat to have Ethan Delaney killed, it was unavoidably necessary. Delaney had saved his life back in Iraq. But David had returned the favor. Besides they weren't in Iraq any more. They were in America and the war here was much more intense than anyone knew. There was so much more to gain here, thus more to lose. And no matter how bloody things got, David intended to win. Nothing or no one was going to get in his way. Delaney would be a formidable opponent, but that would not stop David.

"Is everything all right?"

David looked at the lovely woman at his side. The dinner gown she wore was exquisite. She looked absolutely beautiful wearing the elegant black dress, fully relaxed against the luxurious leather seat. Her long blond hair veiled her slender shoulders like a cape of pure silk. Those blue eyes peered up at him in complete awe. Yes. So beautiful and so perfect.

"Everything is perfect," he told her.

She smiled. "Good."

David draped an arm around his wife's shoulders. Oh, yes. Everything was perfect now.

Nothing could stop him.

# Chapter Four

"Why don't you just admit that I was right," Jenn protested in earnest. "Someone tried to kill me and you know it!"

Ethan took a moment to tamp down his irritation before he answered. "Yes, I do believe someone just tried to kill you." He tossed aside the overnight bag in the cargo area of his Navigator. "Or me...or both of us," he added, surveying the handpicked emergency items he carried with him at all times in what looked like a typical mechanic's toolbox.

She huffed indignantly. "You are the most stubborn man I've ever met." She crossed her arms with exaggerated drama. "I don't understand. You can't be that dense. You have to know those bullets were meant for *me.*"

Ethan turned toward her, allowing her the full measure of his impatience. "Get in the car."

She glared right back at him. "Not until you tell me why you still don't believe me." She lifted that defiant little chin. "We're wasting time, so make it quick."

Reaching for calm, he spoke slowly, allowing no

room for misunderstanding. "I am convinced that someone is trying to harm you. And it most likely is someone from BalPhar, or at the very least someone in the business." He cranked up the intensity of his stare. "But there is no evidence linking David Crane to what's happening. Yet," he qualified for her benefit. "If any exists, I'll find it. Now, get in the car."

She held her ground for a few seconds longer before surrendering to the inevitable. "Fine," she snapped.

To his relief she started to actually obey him, but then hesitated. "What is all that stuff?" she asked, pointing to the toolbox where he'd stored her thirty-eight. There was no telling what kind of crimes it had been used in. He would turn it over to a detective friend in Chicago PD first chance he got.

He cocked his head and grinned at her curiosity. She had just been shot at, manhandled and still she couldn't resist the unknown. "The tools of my trade, little girl."

The evil eye she aimed in his direction only served to widen his grin.

"I am not a little girl," she retorted hotly. "Stop calling me that. You may call me *Dr.* Ballard. I thought we'd already clarified that matter."

"Well, *Dr.* Ballard," he returned, "I have everything here I need to do my job. A couple of extra weapons, ammo, night vision, binoculars, Kevlar vest, just to name a few. Now, will you please get in the car before your friends come back for another round of target practice?"

Her eyes widened with the fear of what she obviously hadn't considered. She pivoted and did as he'd told her what felt like eons ago. Ethan cursed himself as he watched that cute little rear end sway from side to side as she stormed up to the passenger side of the vehicle.

"Mercy," he muttered. His objectivity was definitely going downhill fast. His gut clenched with an undeniably sensual yearning. She might have a body made for loving, he warned the part of him that refused to listen to reason, but she was practically a kid. Too damned young for him.

*And she's your client,* he added with a good, swift mental kick to his sluggish gray matter.

After checking to see that he had everything he thought he would need, Ethan closed the rear doors and strode to the driver's side. He had the perfect place in mind where he could keep her safe. Pierce Maxwell's cabin near Crystal Lake. Max, as he was known to his friends, was out of the country on agency business. Ethan knew where he kept his spare key, just as Max knew where Ethan kept the key to his apartment in the city. The cabin was thirty minutes northwest of the city, deep in the woods where Ethan wouldn't have to worry about being noticed by nosy neighbors or snooping shop owners.

"This isn't a car, you know," Jennifer said as he slid behind the wheel of the vehicle.

Turning the ignition, Ethan looked at her in question. "What?"

Arms still crossed over her perky breasts, she stared straight ahead now. "You called this a car. It isn't a car."

Ethan put the *car* in gear and eased out of the motel

parking lot. The clerk would be relieved to see them go. He'd repeated over and over as Ethan counted out the cash for the damages to their room that he hadn't seen anything and wouldn't remember Ethan after he walked out the door. Of course, that would easily change with the right motivation. That was the reason Ethan would deliberately take a wrong turn and then double back. If asked, the guy would give the wrong information and swear it was gospel.

"I hadn't really thought about it," he said irritably in answer to her annoying observation that his vehicle wasn't a car. "Don't worry about it though." He glanced at his passenger before pulling out onto the highway. "I bought it. I do know what it is. And even more important, I know how to operate it."

She looked away, unimpressed. "Where are we going?"

"To a safe house."

"Where?" she demanded sharply. "I want to be kept informed of *our* plans."

She was the most demanding woman he'd ever had the unfortunate experience of protecting. "Northwest of Chicago, near Crystal Lake. Don't worry," he went on at her startled gasp, "we're not going anywhere near BalPhar or Aurora."

"But what are we going to do?" she wanted to know then. "We have to do something to stop David."

He sighed. It was almost dark already, and he was tired. Too tired to play twenty questions. "All you have to know is that I'm on the job." He stopped for a red light, taking the opportunity to look directly into her eyes. "You don't have to worry that pretty little head of yours about any of this. I'll take care of everything. Right now the only thing we have to do is go someplace safe."

Indignation sent her chin up a notch. "I want to know exactly what you have planned up front. We're not doing anything without my approval."

Oh-ho. Little Miss Senior Vice President was used to having things her way. Maybe that's why Crane was trying to get rid of her, Ethan mused sardonically. He slammed the brakes on that line of thinking. He was letting her get to him…he couldn't allow that. She could be the victim here. No matter how brave she appeared, deep down he knew she was scared to death. She only wanted to understand what was happening around her. It was just difficult for him to sympathize given the circumstances. He still didn't know for absolute certain who she was, or what she was actually up to. And he damned sure didn't know if Crane was involved.

"When we arrive at our destination, we'll talk about what steps to take next. Fair enough?"

"Fair enough." She met the assurance in his eyes with lead in her own. "Just make sure you don't try to pull a fast one. I don't plan to let another man take advantage of me."

Ethan blinked, focusing his attention forward as the light turned green. He hadn't considered how having her fiancé order her execution had made her feel about men. He frowned. Then again, at this point, he wasn't even sure she'd been engaged, much less to David Crane.

"You have nothing to worry about," he intoned. "I would never take advantage of anyone, certainly not—"

"I swear," she broke in, "if you call me a little girl again, I'll scream."

"I was going to say," he said tightly, "a woman already afraid for her life." It was a lie, but she didn't have to know. *Little girl* was exactly what he'd intended to say. Well, he mused, if he really considered her a little girl, what the hell did that make him? A dirty old man?

"Why don't you get some sleep? I'll wake you up when we get there. It's an hour or so from here."

"I'm not tired." She squared her shoulders and stared straight ahead.

"Suit yourself." She was the one lying this time. The dark circles under those big blue eyes shouted exhaustion. She was probably hungry again, too, but wouldn't admit it. He'd pick up something at a drive-thru before going to Max's place. With Max out of the country, his kitchen might be less than well stocked.

Once on the interstate Ethan relaxed into the seat and set the cruise control. He glanced at Jennifer Ballard. Already she was struggling to keep her eyes open. She definitely was not a very good liar. What did that say about her accusations against Crane?

That she truly believed him to be the enemy.

Maybe.

Still, that didn't quite sit right with Ethan. Maybe

he'd made a mistake by taking this assignment. Maybe Victoria had been right about the past getting in the way. But Ethan wasn't ready to admit defeat just yet. If he discovered that Crane was involved, he would handle the situation. He'd never once allowed personal feelings to get in the way of his job.

An all too vivid image from the past slammed into his mind disputing his claim.

He had made a mistake once. And once had been enough. He would never allow that to happen again. If David Crane was guilty, he would go down.

A lot could change in eight years. Drug research was big business…big money. Greed could change a man. In Ethan's experience, following the money usually led to the person calling the shots. In this situation, Crane would be the most likely suspect. He would have the most to gain by Jennifer's absence, thus putting him in the decision-making seat. Then again, if they weren't married, what did he actually stand to gain in the long run?

Not much to Ethan's way of thinking. So what if he had control at that moment? Jennifer would have no problem regaining power once her identity was established. Well, Ethan amended, barring any mental instability. That reminded him. He had a few calls to make. He needed to talk to Victoria, give her an update, then one to Melbourne and another to Amy Wells. Amy, though a little taller, was about the same size as Jennifer. She could drop some clothes off at the cabin.

Ethan glanced at the ragged jeans and the too-short top his client, who was now asleep, wore. His throat instantly parched as his gaze roved over her bare midriff, then traced the curve of her breast. He jerked his attention back to the long ribbon of highway. He hadn't had this much trouble keeping his mind off sex since he was a teenager.

She's nothing but a kid, he told himself yet again. "Just a little girl," he muttered.

"I am not a little girl," she corrected without opening her eyes. Her soft voice was thick with exhaustion, but undeniably firm.

Ethan shook his head. It was going to be a very long night.

"JENNIFER."

Jenn jerked awake.

It was dark.

Horror exploded inside her. She had to get away. She scrambled to escape the hands touching her. She rammed into something hard…a door.

"Jennifer! It's me, Ethan." His fingers tightened around her upper arms. "Wake up. You're safe now."

She was with Delaney…in his SUV. She was safe.

If only that were true.

Slumping with the receding adrenaline, Jenn shrugged off his hands. "I'm awake."

He opened the driver's-side door and got out. She fumbled around until she found the lever for her own door, then clambered out. She felt disoriented for a couple of moments, but quickly steadied herself. A light was on inside the small A-frame house nestled in the wooded landscape. The dim illumination didn't quite reach the dark deck. The man who'd brought her here came around to her side of the vehicle. The click of locking doors echoed when he pressed the remote on his key chain. The sound made her shiver. Could she really trust this man?

She couldn't think that way. She had to trust someone.

Jenn glanced up and briefly admired the full moon. It cast a golden glow over the forest that seemed to swallow them up as they walked closer to the house. It annoyed her that she had fallen asleep. She had no idea where she was. The Crystal Lake area was unfamiliar to her. She'd never be able to get out of here on her own. She glared at Delaney's broad back as he led the way. She was stuck with him. It might as well be him she trusted.

And he hadn't even decided if he believed her yet.

Near the front deck, he drifted to the right and disappeared in the shadows at the end of the house. Her legs suddenly paralyzed, Jenn froze on the stone walk. He was gone. She squinted in an attempt to see him in the darkness. She hated the dark. Those minutes in the motel room with the drapes pulled and the lights out had been pure torture.

"Where are you?" she asked, her voice small, frightened. She shivered. Where the hell was he?

"Right here."

She jumped when he came up right beside her. "Damn! What're you trying to do? Give me a heart attack?"

He grinned with that devilish, yet wry twisting of his

lips that made her stomach quiver. "You're too young to have a heart attack." He marched up the walk and onto the deck apparently expecting her to follow.

There he went with that age thing again. What was it with this guy and age? He didn't look old. Who even cared? She trudged after him. At least she could take a long hot bath now. She'd been afraid to let her guard down long enough at the motel to do anything other than take a quick shower. A cold one at that.

"I thought you said we were going to a safe house," she protested, suddenly remembering his words, as he let himself through the door and then stepped aside for her to enter. "Where are the security walls and armed personnel?"

He closed and locked the door behind her. "You've seen too many movies." He looked at her then, really looked at her, as if trying to see inside her, or maybe make her see what was inside him. "Trust me, this place is secure." He punched a code into the keypad on the wall next to the door. "It belongs to a friend of mine, Max."

The presence of a security system made her feel marginally better. But the fact that they were out in the boonies still made her uneasy.

"You stay here while I take a quick look around," he ordered, dropping the bag he'd brought inside from the SUV on the shiny hardwood floor.

Waffling between following him and staying put, she looked from his retreating back to the bag he'd abandoned on the floor. Did he have more weapons in there?

He'd taken a couple of things from the toolbox and put them inside the bag. What else did he carry in there?

Determined to know more about the man in whose hands her life rested, she knelt next to the bag and quickly unzipped it. A forbidding weapon, a couple of loaded ammo clips, jeans, shirt, socks, underwear. She lifted a skeptical eyebrow at the undergarment. Nothing like her father wore.

She jerked her hand back as if she'd touched his body instead of just his briefs. Okay, so he wasn't packing anything to be concerned about, like interrogation torture devices. It was a simple overnight bag with a big, wicked-looking gun inside. That's all.

"Find anything interesting?"

Her head came up. He was glaring down at her from two feet away. How had he sneaked up on her like that? He'd done the same thing outside.

"I was just…just looking to see if you had anything in there I could wear." She tugged at her barely there top. "This is not exactly me."

"Follow me," he said as he turned toward the stairs. His impatience had clearly peaked.

Feigning humble obedience, Jenn rose from her kneeling position and followed him up the narrow staircase. The second-floor landing spilled into a large master suite. The furnishings were spartan, other than the bed, which was a massive four-poster. The decorating was late nineties, single male. Not really bad, just lean. The log and chink walls were completely unadorned. The comforter on the bed was beige in color, thick and inviting. There was more workout equipment than actual furniture in the room. This Max fellow was apparently an exercise freak.

"I had a friend drop off a few things you might need." Delaney gestured to the soft-sided suitcase sitting at the foot of the bed. "If you need anything else, just let me know and I'll have Amy drop it by."

*Amy?* "Who's Amy?" she asked, immediately hating that she'd done so, especially considering something akin to jealousy barbed her the instant he spoke the woman's name. Was Amy his girlfriend? His wife? He didn't wear a ring. Why did she care? She reflected with growing unease on the direction her thoughts were taking.

"Amy's with the agency, too," he explained, then backed toward the stairs. "Let me know if you need anything else. I'll be downstairs."

Jenn frowned. "Where will you sleep?" Just another thing that shouldn't matter one iota to her. But she hadn't seen a bedroom downstairs. There was a large great room and a doorway that led into what looked like a kitchen and a closed door tucked in one corner that might be a powder room, but definitely no bedroom.

"Downstairs," he said. "Couch." He turned and descended the stairs without a backward glance.

Too tired to analyze his rush to get away from her, she opened the suitcase and rummaged through the contents. A couple pair of jeans, a T-shirt, two blouses, socks, sneakers and panties. She arched an eyebrow. A bra? She checked the size—it was hers. How had this Amy managed that little feat?

Heat flushed her cheeks at the notion that Delaney

had accurately estimated the size. The idea that he'd looked at her that closely prompted a tingling low in her belly. She forced her attention back to the contents of the bag. A nightshirt, toothbrush and toothpaste, and a few other cosmetics. Oh, heavenly. She couldn't wait to brush her teeth with something other than her finger and water.

Grabbing the things she would need for a bath, she headed for the bathroom. Ten minutes later she was soaking in neck-deep water. The tub was huge. She loved it. She owed Delaney for this, big-time. As the minutes ticked by the hot water slowly dissolved the tension in her aching body. She was so tired. She squeezed her eyes shut and tried not to think about her father. What if she didn't get to see him again?

Please, she prayed, keep my father safe from David. And please, God, don't let him die before I get home again.

She forced back the tears and focused on washing her hair and body. The sooner she was finished, the sooner she could get to sleep. She needed her rest. Tomorrow she had to find a way to prove who she was and what David Crane was up to.

As she dried her hair and skin with a towel, she considered that maybe it was time she played her trump card. It was abundantly clear that she hadn't convinced Delaney with her explanation of her plight.

She'd worried that she might be making a mistake if she let that particular cat out of the bag too soon since she had nothing readily available to prove her case. But it was evident now that drastic measures were called for. Tomorrow morning she would make sure Ethan Delaney saw for himself what she was really up against…why she couldn't go to the police.

Maybe that would convince the man that she was telling the truth. She wrapped the towel around her, tucking one end between her breasts.

Then again, she mused, it could backfire. Work exactly the opposite way. She definitely didn't need that.

Whatever happened, she had to do it. She couldn't put it off any longer.

Midway to the bed Jenn halted abruptly as Delaney suddenly appeared at the top of the staircase. She gasped. He looked as startled as she was.

"I…ah…brought you dinner." He nodded to the tray in his hands.

A bottle of water and a bottle of beer sat next to a fast-food bag on the tray. He'd stopped at a restaurant on the way here and she hadn't even known, she'd slept so soundly. Squaring her shoulders, she crossed the room and took the tray from him.

"I didn't know which you preferred, beer or water. There wasn't anything else."

"Thank you," she said as if nothing at all was out of sync. She didn't miss the way his gaze swept down her half-naked body, lingered on her bare legs, then whipped back up to her face. Nor did she miss the flare of heat in his eyes.

"You're welcome." He moistened his lips. "Like I said, I'll be right downstairs if you need anything."

"Good night, Mr. Delaney," she said with a scarcely

maintained smile. The way he'd looked at her was completely unnerving.

"Good night, Jenn—Dr. Ballard."

She tried not to visually measure his shoulders as he descended the stairs. She'd already thoroughly examined his too-perfect gluteus maximus. She hated that she noticed anything about him, especially the way he looked at her.

Enlightenment dawned. He was attracted to her, too. She felt suddenly giddy, foolishly so. She hurried to the bed and set the tray down. She forced herself to consider this new development more objectively. That could prove her ticket to staying in control. All she had to do was keep him unsteady and he'd be a lot easier to handle. She'd never attempted that tactic before, but sultry women always did it in the movies.

Grinning in triumph, she sauntered over to the railing that overlooked the great room. "Mr. Delaney," she called to her bodyguard who was now draped languidly across the couch, a bottle of water in his hand. He'd taken off his shirt. She swallowed convulsively, struggled for composure. How could any chest look that good? Especially from this distance?

He looked up at her. "Yeah?"

"Exactly how old are you?" She braced her hands on the wooden railing and leaned forward slightly in hopes of looking seductive. She hadn't actually tried before so she couldn't be sure if she was doing it right.

"Why do you ask?" Uncertainty plagued his tone.

Good. It was working. "Oh," she purred, "I don't know. Just curious." She reached up then and released her hair from its makeshift bun. The long, still slightly damp tresses spilled over her shoulders.

"Thirty-four," he said flatly.

She considered that for a moment, pretending to do the math. "Okay." She whirled around and sashayed back to the bed, out of his field of vision.

She plopped down on the covers and dove into the burger and fries he'd brought her. She took a long swallow of her bottled water and then smiled.

Oh, yes. She had Mr. Delaney now. Though it was far from customary for her, she would use this little attraction to her benefit. She had, after all, learned from the best. David Crane was a master manipulator. The tragic lesson she'd endured at his hand should prove worth something.

Now, all she needed was a foolproof plan for tomorrow morning.

AT EIGHT the next morning Ethan shook his head grimly. He couldn't believe he'd allowed her to talk him into this.

"It's a good thing you had those binoculars," Jennifer Ballard noted aloud, her tone entirely too chipper.

Ethan glared at her. "I'm always prepared."

"Just like a Boy Scout," she said teasingly.

She smiled then. The same way she had last night while clad only in a towel. His gut clenched. Dammit. He looked away, lifted the binoculars back to his eyes and surveyed the front of the Ballard mansion yet again. This was ridiculous.

"What the hell am I looking for?" he snapped, lowering the binoculars far enough to glare at her once more. Was it his imagination or was she trying to get to him?

"Trust me," she said, repeating his words from yesterday. "You'll know it when you see it."

He had lost his mind. There could be no doubt. Otherwise he wouldn't be parked on a service road adjacent to Austin Ballard's house, his vehicle camouflaged by trees and bushes. But she'd insisted that if they came here this morning and watched David Crane exit the Ballard residence on his way to work, then Ethan would understand why she couldn't go to the police.

As the minutes ticked by, he grew more and more certain of one thing—she was as nutty as a fruitcake. Young and beautiful, but a couple of cards shy of a full deck. Though she'd been right to a point. When he'd checked in with Victoria, he'd learned that David Crane and Jennifer Ballard had, in fact, applied for a marriage license.

"He's coming out," she said. She grabbed Ethan by the arm and shook him, just in case he missed her announcement.

Annoyed, he stared through the damned binoculars. What the hell did she expect him to see? David Crane walked out of the house, briefcase in hand. The fact that he exited the Ballard residence didn't really bother Ethan. For all he knew Crane could be stopping by to check on the old man.

Crane moved down the steps, but hesitated before climbing into the waiting car. He looked back up at the door he'd exited only moments before. Ethan followed his gaze. A woman came out and started down the steps.

Everything inside Ethan stilled as he watched the woman walk toward David Crane.

Nothing could have prepared him for this.

He couldn't believe his eyes.

He squeezed them tightly shut for a second, then peered through the magnifying lenses again.

The woman now at Crane's side was the exact double of the woman sitting in the car next to Ethan. It was like looking at the spitting image of the very one who'd haunted his sleep last night.

When Crane and the woman had gotten into the car, Ethan lowered the binoculars and looked at the woman beside him. "Who the hell is she?"

Jennifer shrugged. "Don't ask me. All I can tell you is that she's not Jennifer Ballard, because I am."

# Chapter Five

"She's stolen my whole life," Jenn murmured as she stared at the front page of the *Chicago Tribune* a little later that morning. A picture of David and the impostor was plastered across the page. The headline read Daughter of Pharmaceuticals Magnate Weds Research Pioneer in Private Ceremony. The whole world thought the woman in the picture was Jenn, but it wasn't. She was here…robbed of all that she was.

"Why would Crane go to these lengths?" Delaney wanted to know. He'd picked up the day's paper at a convenience store on their way back to the cabin. "This is a little farfetched, you have to admit."

He still didn't believe her.

"I'm telling you he killed Russ because he knew something was wrong with the Kessler Project. Uncle Russ warned me before he died so now I'm in David's way, too. If he'd murder a man in cold blood, this—" she shoved the paper at Ethan "—would be a piece of cake."

"Okay, let's say for the moment he masterminded this look-alike business to cover your absence after he killed you." He tossed the paper aside. "To what end? He was already in charge of the Kessler Project. And if—" he said when she would have interrupted "—he's hiding something, what is it? What exactly is wrong with the Kessler Project?" he challenged as he poured himself a second cup of coffee. "We have to have more than speculation here."

How on earth did she convince this guy? He was playing devil's advocate to the extreme, refuting everything she said. Trying to be rational when there was nothing rational about any of this. Jenn sank into a chair at the kitchen table and stared at her own untouched coffee. The whole situation was hopeless. She was holed up out here in the woods while some other woman lived her life.

"I don't have all the answers. I can only assume that he wants control of the whole company. He knew once we were married I'd step aside since I prefer the research over the management, but Russ ruined that plan." She shrugged. "As far as the Kessler Project, Russ didn't have time to tell me anything specific before he died. Just the warning that something was wrong with the Kessler Project and that David had lied." She closed her eyes to block out the memory of the horror in his face…all the blood. The crimson trail down the front of her pristine white wedding dress. She squeezed her eyes shut, shattering the images.

An epiphany of sorts made her laugh, but the sound held no humor. "What's really pathetic is that I would probably still have trusted David—even after what Russ told me—if I hadn't heard with my own ears when he ordered that man to kill me. I was that blind.''

"How do we find out what's wrong with the Kessler Project?'' Delaney pulled a chair from the table, sat down astride it, then propped his arms, cup of coffee in hand, on the back of it.

Jenn feathered her fingers through her hair and absently wished for some pins with which to put it up out of her way. She never wore it down like this. She glanced around the unfamiliar kitchen belonging to Delaney's friend, then down at the borrowed clothes she wore. Her existence had been so controlled, sheltered really, until now. Her father had always assured that everything was as he desired. But now he couldn't help her. How could one man have so much power that he could steal her whole life? It just seemed impossible that she could be here now with no way to prove who she was or to get her life back.

Had she depended so much on her father her entire life that now she couldn't help herself? Panic burgeoned inside her. Wait, she told herself, she'd made it this far on her own. No one had been there to tell her what to do after she'd escaped David's henchman. She'd gotten the gun, the clothes and the bus ticket all by herself. She'd called the Colby Agency. She frowned. The jury was still out on that decision. Perhaps calling Victoria Colby hadn't been such a stroke of genius after all.

"Jennifer," Delaney said, tugging her back to the here and now. "Is there a way to remote access the BalPhar files?''

She shook her head. "All incoming lines are secure.

No one gets in online. And even if someone managed, the electronic security is unbreachable."

"No system is unbreachable," Delaney challenged. He sipped his coffee, those dark eyes watching her over the rim of his cup.

Jenn pushed out of her chair and started to pace. She didn't like it when he looked at her that way. Analyzing, trying to see inside her head. "Well," she said flippantly. "Since we don't have a resident hacker here to help us figure out a way in electronically—" she planted her hands on her hips and stared directly at Delaney "—we'll just have to wait until after midnight when most everyone is gone and walk in through the front door. I have to have irrefutable proof that I'm Jennifer Ballard."

"That's a little risky, don't you think?" He set his cup aside as if the contents no longer held any interest for him. She knew how that felt. "For someone who didn't even want to go near the place just a few hours ago."

She swallowed the fear pressing against the back of her throat. "I don't see any other way. It's my only hope. Every minute we waste is another one I won't get to spend with my father." She blinked back the moisture welling in her eyes.

"What about dental records?"

Jenn shook her head. "My dentist's office conveniently burned down."

Ethan sighed. "There has to be another way."

She shook her head solemnly. "That's the only way." She paused and looked across the table at him.

Would he help her? As usual, his long hair was pulled back and secured at his nape. The small silver hoop in his left ear distracted her for a moment. She suddenly wondered where the tattoo would be? She shivered and looked away. Were all Colby Agents this roguish looking? "We have to get inside," she told him, focusing on the problem at hand. "That's the bottom line. And even that's no good if David has already destroyed any incriminating evidence." God, she'd only just thought of that. Would he destroy all the files…everything that proved she was who she said she was? She had the sudden, unbidden feeling that time was swiftly running out for her. A sinking feeling threatened her composure. This was hopeless.

"What about Kessler? Would he talk?"

Jenn frowned. "I don't know." She walked over to the sink, leaned against the counter and stared out the window. "Maybe not to me. His parting of ways with BalPhar was not amicable. He blames my father for allowing David to take over the project. If he knows anything important, he might not want to share it with me."

Delaney stood and walked in her direction, drawing her attention to him, or more specifically to his body, once more. She tried not to observe so closely the way he moved, but she just couldn't help herself. He was so fluid, so graceful for such a large man. There was something mesmerizing about it. She railed at herself inwardly. She was supposed to be leading him around by the nose, not the other way around.

"It's worth a shot." He paused a couple of feet away

and leaned one elbow on the counter to put himself more at eye level with her, she supposed. "I'm surprised that Crane, if he's really behind all this, hasn't tied up that loose end already."

Jenn felt the blood drain from her face. She hadn't thought of that, either. If David was tying up loose ends, the way he'd done with Russ, then Kessler might be next. Might even already be dead. He was the only evidence she had on the outside. She had to get to him before David did.

She glanced at the digital clock on the microwave. "If we leave right now, we could be at his house before lunch."

Delaney blocked her way when she would have moved. "There's something else we have to talk about first," he told her.

She looked up at him. God, he was tall, with shoulders that went on forever. "We don't have time to talk."

He didn't budge. "What about the woman, Jenn?" He seemed suddenly closer somehow. "You're asking me to suspend belief here. To take your word that you're Jennifer Ballard and that the woman I saw walk out of the Ballard home was an impostor. You must know how this looks."

So that's why he hadn't pushed the subject when they'd left her house. He'd decided she was the impostor and he wanted to wait until he had her safely back here to present the idea.

Had David gotten to him during their meeting yesterday?

Fury ignited inside her. "Forget you, Delaney. I'll go to Kessler on my own. I shouldn't have called the Colby Agency." She tried to push past him, but he held her back, strong fingers closing around her arms.

"You're not going anywhere without me," he said softly, but firmly. "If you believe your life is in danger, then striking out on your own would not be a wise move."

She struggled against his iron grip. *"If?"* She glared at him. "How can you still say if? Those bullets yesterday were meant for me and you know it."

"I agree. It's *you* that doesn't seem to believe it or you surely wouldn't consider walking away from the only help available to you."

The fight leeched out of her. He was right. She didn't have any transportation or money. What could she do alone? "I can't prove who I am. What do you want from me?" she demanded, her eyes filling with emotion. She hated that, she didn't want to cry. "I could tell you all about my childhood, but what would that prove? The one person who could corroborate my stories rarely has moments where he's able to communicate." God, she wanted to go home. To sit beside her father's bed and will him back to good health.

"I'm not saying I don't believe you. I'm looking at this the way the police will. Crane has probably already considered you might go to the authorities. He could claim you're a disgruntled former employee who just happens to look a lot like his wife." He released her as if he'd only just realized he was still holding her. "Hell, he might even say you're a long-lost family member out for revenge or control of the Ballard fortune.''

She looked up at him, those big blue eyes liquid. ''There is no one.''

''Think,'' Delaney urged. ''Is there any possibility that you know her? Could she be related to you?''

Jenn shook her head. She was so tired and confused. She just wanted to go home…to make all this go away. ''I've never seen her before. It has to be some sort of trick. Cosmetic surgery, something. *I don't know the woman.*''

''One more thing,'' he said gently, so gently it surprised her, made her feel even more vulnerable.

She looked up at him and tried to read what she saw in his eyes, but couldn't. ''What?''

''Is there any chance your father could have been involved in what Kessler recognized as wrong?''

''No!'' How dare he even suggest such a thing! ''My father and I are the victims here. Why can't I get that across to you? If you're not here to help me, then why not just take me back to where you found me and stop pretending my dilemma matters to you?'' She was shaking, and she hated that even worse than crying. She didn't want to appear weak. She had to be strong. Seeing her father again depended upon what she did right now. Who knew what the woman posing as her could do…could already have done to hurt her father? Renewed panic surged inside her.

''All right,'' he relented, though she couldn't be sure whether he believed her or if he just feared a crying jag. "We'll assume for the moment that everything you've said is true. Now we have to prove it."

"We have to get to Kessler before David does," she said, choosing to ignore his use of the word *assume*. "There's no more time for discussing or arguing."

"I couldn't have said it better."

He released her and walked out of the kitchen. To make preparations to go, she presumed. She shook her head. Was she finally making headway with him? Or was he simply desperate to shut her up? Probably the latter.

One thing was certain, the burden of proof was on her.

"THE NEXT RIGHT."

Ethan made the turn, then glanced at his passenger. She'd been quiet most of the trip. That worried him. If she wasn't talking, that meant she was thinking. That, in his short experience with her, spelled trouble.

The few seconds he'd watched through the binoculars this morning as the other woman emerged from the Ballard home instantly replayed in his mind. The woman didn't just look like Jennifer Ballard, she was an exact double, on the surface anyway. Height, weight and even her posture appeared the same. It was like looking at an identical twin. But Jennifer Ballard had no siblings and wasn't adopted. The woman had to have been surgically altered to look like the real Jennifer Ballard. She could have studied videotapes or even watched Jennifer to get the posture right. Hair dye and colored contacts could explain the other small details.

That was assuming the woman in the vehicle with him at the moment was the real Jennifer Ballard. The possibility that she wasn't no longer held any merit as far as Ethan was concerned. The motivation it would take for someone to go to these extremes was unfathomable. What could the woman next to him hope to accomplish? The only feasible possibility would be that she was working for a competitor. But why come to the Colby Agency if that was the case? It didn't make sense.

"He's here," she announced. The excitement in her voice drew Ethan back to the present. "That's his car." She pointed to the gray sedan parked near the front of the house. "I just hope he'll talk to us."

Ethan parked a few feet away from the other vehicle. They hadn't called ahead just in case Kessler was skittish.

"I'm going to the door first to check things out. You stay put."

She started to argue, as was her nature it seemed, but thought better of it when he iced her down with a slow stare.

He hesitated before closing his door. "Do you know if he keeps any firearms in the house?"

She shrugged. "Not that I know of. I'm not sure he would even know how to use one."

Ethan didn't feel particularly comforted by that news. The man may have changed a lot in the last year, especially considering his feud with BalPhar.

As he walked slowly to the front door, Ethan scanned the empty yard for any sign of an unexpected welcoming committee. Nothing. The property was a ways off the beaten path. Not quite in the sticks, but close. The residence was a two-story frame farmhouse, white with classic green shutters. There was a slightly more modern detached garage and another building, somewhat larger and even newer looking than the garage. Drawing closer to the house, he noted the security keypad next to the door leading into the other building that sat between the garage and the house. Since Kessler was a scientist, Ethan supposed it was a laboratory, especially considering it appeared to have high-tech security and the house did not. The lack of windows was also telling.

The noonday sun beat down unusually harshly today. Ethan felt a line of perspiration forming on his brow. He listened for signs of life. A near-nonexistent breeze stirred the air just enough to rustle the leaves. A bird flitted from limb to limb in a massive oak that shaded the porch. Gravel crunched beneath Ethan's boots. When he reached the wooden steps leading to the wrap-around porch, he paused and listened intently for any sounds coming from inside the house. The front door was open, with only a screen door shielding the entrance. The up-to-date dark tint of the screen concealed all that lay beyond it and indicated the owner had taken some steps to preserve his privacy.

Just as Ethan lifted his right foot toward the first step, the unmistakable ratchet of a pump shotgun froze him in place.

"This is private property."

Ethan peered at the screened door, but could only make out a vague shadow behind it. The voice that had come from beyond it was definitely male, probably an older man. Kessler, he hoped. "My name is Ethan Delaney. I'm with the Colby Agency. I'd like to speak with you. It's rather urgent."

"Take out your ID and hold it open where I can see it. Then I want both your hands up in the air."

"It's inside my jacket. I'll have to reach—"

"Take off your jacket!"

Ethan could hear the rising anxiety in the man's voice. The last thing he wanted was a panicked scientist holding a cocked shotgun aimed at him.

"No problem," Ethan assured him. "But first I need to know if you're Lawrence Kessler."

"That depends on what you want."

Ethan took that as a yes. He carefully tugged off the jacket and draped it across the steps, then reached inside the interior pocket and retrieved his ID.

"I know you're carrying a gun," Kessler said pointedly. "Put it down where I can see it as well."

Cautious old fellow, Ethan thought. "Sure thing. Just stay calm, my friend," he placated as he reached behind him and removed the gun from his waistband. He laid the weapon on his jacket, hoping that the old man wouldn't be savvy enough to think of an ankle holster. "Are we cool now?"

The screen door swung open and the old man stepped out onto the porch, a twelve-gauge double-barrelled shotgun in his hands. He peered at Ethan's credentials without ever lowering the bead on Ethan's chest. "What does the Colby Agency want with me?" Kessler demanded gruffly.

"I just need to ask you a couple of questions," Ethan explained. "Don't worry, I'm not working for Bal-Phar."

Startled at hearing that name, Kessler looked even more uncertain as to whether Ethan was friend or foe. "You've got one minute to convince me not to shoot you," the old man warned.

Before Ethan could offer further explanation, the closing of a vehicle door jerked both his and Kessler's attention toward the Navigator. Jennifer was striding toward the house.

Ethan swore under his breath.

"Not working for BalPhar, huh?" the old man growled. "Don't come any closer!" he warned the woman approaching. "I've got nothing to say to you."

"Look," Ethan said calmly. "Give us a chance to explain."

"I said, don't come any closer!" he shouted at Jennifer.

"Listen to him," Ethan growled. To his relief she stopped...only to do something much worse.

"Dr. Kessler, I know there's something wrong with Cellneu. I need you to tell me what it is," she called out to him, her tone almost accusing.

Ethan swore again. If she didn't get them both killed it would be a miracle...or only that Kessler couldn't hit the broad side of a barn.

"It's nothing I did," Kessler shouted back, a new tension in his voice. "I tried to tell them, but they wouldn't listen. Ballard should have known better, but he took Crane's word over mine! Whatever goes wrong serves him right.''

Silence ruled for several long beats. Ethan considered going for the gun or maybe the .22 in the ankle holster, but even if Kessler was a lousy shot, this close there was bound to be some damage.

''In two weeks they're starting testing on a control group of human subjects,'' Jennifer told him, her voice strained, shaky almost. ''Cellneu is slated for full approval by the FDA before the end of the year.''

''Fools,'' Kessler muttered. ''I'm no longer responsible. I did all I could to stop it. I have a daughter in Colorado. I won't risk her and her family. Don't ask me to.''

''Did someone threaten you, Dr. Kessler?'' Ethan asked quietly.

Kessler laughed, a dry, humorless sound. ''Oh, not in so many words, but I got the message loud and clear.''

''I need your help, Dr. Kessler,'' Jennifer urged.

She stood right next to Ethan now. He had to refrain from grabbing her by the arms and shaking the hell out of her. Any sudden moves from either one of them might be interpreted by Kessler as aggression.

''Just leave me alone,'' the old man ground out. ''I've got my own work now.''

''Dr. Kessler, I know my father made a mistake. I wonder now if it had anything to do with his illness. His health has deteriorated very rapidly this last year. We don't know exactly what it is yet. But it may have affected his judgment at the time he took David's side over yours.''

Kessler weighed her words. He lowered the weapon he held in a death grip. "People will die if they go forward with Cellneu.''

"Tell us how to stop them,'' Jennifer pleaded.

"We have to have evidence,'' Ethan interjected. "If we bring down whoever is responsible for this, your family will be safe. Right now, they're not really safe and neither are you.''

"It's Crane,'' Kessler growled. "Don't doubt it. He's money- and power-hungry. He doesn't care about anything else. Greedy son of a bitch.''

Ethan suffered a moment of regret.

Jennifer glowered at him. "I told you. When are you going to start believing me?''

Ethan said to Kessler, "If we could come inside and discuss this further, your help might be instrumental in making this right.''

Kessler exhaled a heavy breath. "All right. Come in.'' He held the screen door open for them, all the while scanning warily to make sure no one else was around.

Ethan followed Jennifer into the shadowy living room. The shades were pulled tight. Kessler propped his shotgun in a corner and then turned on a table lamp.

He gestured to the sofa. "Please, sit down.''

Ethan waited for Jennifer to take a seat, but she was as preoccupied as Ethan with their surroundings. The room looked like a shrine. Pictures of a woman during various stages of her life were everywhere, as were flowers and candles. Mrs. Kessler, Ethan presumed.

"How is Mrs. Kessler?" Jennifer asked, confirming his estimation. She surveyed the single-minded decor once more as she waited for his response.

Kessler, still standing, glanced about the room, sadness visibly overtaking him. "She died six months ago."

"I'm so sorry," Jennifer offered.

"Cancer," Kessler said, his voice hollow.

Ethan wondered if Jennifer was thinking about the drug, Cellneu. Would that drug have helped Kessler's wife if it had been safe to use?

"Do you know how badly I wanted to treat her with Cellneu?" Kessler asked, as if reading Ethan's mind.

The pain in his voice made Ethan's gut clench.

"You're that certain that it's not safe for humans?" Jennifer wanted to know.

Kessler nodded. "It appears to be perfectly safe at first, and the results are astounding. But it causes irreversible changes in certain cells."

"Genetic alterations," Jennifer murmured, her expression solemn. "God. How did we miss that?"

Kessler shook his head. "It's not apparent at first. The changed cells are dormant for months. That's how we missed it. When I discovered it, I tried to stop them, but no one would listen. Crane insisted that the incidence would be minimal. That the good would far outweigh the bad."

Ethan looked from one scientist to the other. "What happens when those cells wake up?"

"They destroy everything in their path," Kessler said. "Death is inevitable."

"If David has his way—" Jennifer directed this at Ethan "—the drug will be released to thousands of people." Her eyes grew wide with the full realization of her own words. "Imagine how many will die."

"Is it possible that Crane is right about the low incidence?" Ethan prodded. He had to be sure about the man. The charges were serious ones. The man Ethan remembered had had visions of saving the world. He'd shared that dream during those seventy-two hours in hell with Ethan.

"The incidence of deaths will be far greater than that of survival. Crane knows."

Something in the old man's eyes assured Ethan he was telling the truth. A weight formed in Ethan's gut. His gaze instantly sought Jennifer. Her eyes relayed the same sad finality as Kessler's. Had Crane cruelly ordered the death of the woman he supposedly loved and planned to marry? A girl so young and naive in the ways of the world? She'd been protected her entire life only to get the kind of wake-up call no one deserved.

The sickening reality crashed into Ethan like a jet bursting past the sound barrier.

The look-alike...where had Crane gotten her? How long had he planned that tactic? From what Ethan could surmise, Crane had intended to marry Jennifer Ballard. Russ Gardner's sudden change of heart or his discovery had been the only glitch in the plan. The look-alike must have been a backup, a plan B in the event things went south.

Still, Ethan had a difficult time believing Crane would go to such extremes for control. What had happened to him?

Greed, no doubt. *Money- and power-hungry,* Kessler's words echoed in Ethan's ears. But Ethan had to have proof. One didn't take a man down without indisputable proof.

"We need evidence," Ethan reminded the two, already planning Crane's downfall.

Jennifer stared at him, appalled. "How can you still not be convinced? Haven't you heard enough? *People will die!*"

Ethan fixed her with a determined gaze. "Our hands are tied without proof. You know that as well as I do. You don't bring a guy like Crane down on hearsay. Especially from a former peer who may have revenge on his mind." He glanced at Kessler. "We have to look at this the way the authorities will." He turned back to Jennifer then. "Are you a jilted lover or a concerned scientist?"

Fury blazed in those blue eyes. "Fine." She turned to Kessler. "Do you have any record of your findings?"

Kessler smiled. "I've always believed in the principle of CYA, my dear."

Ethan could definitely relate to that. He liked to cover his as well. "Show us what you've got," he suggested.

"All right." The old man shuffled toward the door. "I have everything hidden away in my lab. I'll bring the file to you. Just wait here. I don't allow visitors in my lab."

"Dr. Kessler," Jennifer said, stopping him at the door. He glanced back at her.

"Thank you," she said. "Thank you for helping us."

He nodded then hurried out the door, allowing the screen to bang behind him.

"I suppose you believe me now," Jennifer said shortly. She pushed to her feet and started her usual routine of pacing the room.

Ethan stood as well. Something niggled at him... something he couldn't quite name. He didn't doubt Kessler's word or his motivation. Hell, he didn't even doubt his client's at this point. The man had watched his own wife die. Had Cellneu been the savior Crane touted, Kessler would certainly have used it to save her. But something didn't feel right. It was that restless sensation that always plagued him when things were about to get worse.

"Maybe we should give Kessler a hand," Ethan suggested.

Jennifer frowned, annoyed or impatient. "But he said to stay here."

Ethan glanced heavenward. Like she'd ever let that stop her before. "I just think—"

A ground-shaking explosion cut off his next words.

"What was that?" Jennifer was attached like a clinging vine to his side now, fear quaking in her voice.

"Stay behind me," Ethan barked as he headed toward the door.

For the first time since he'd found her in that seedy motel room, she obeyed him without question. She clung to his arm and, judging by her grasp, was determined not to let go. Outside, the smell of devastation was already thick in the air. Flames and smoke had engulfed the laboratory.

"Get in the car!" Ethan ordered. He had to try and save Kessler. She'd be safest in the car.

Jennifer stood paralyzed. The laboratory was on fire. Dr. Kessler was in there.

Oh, God.

She told her body to move, but nothing happened.

Ethan ran toward the blazing building. Her heart raced as she watched him slam his shoulder against the intact door that appeared to be the only entry into the building. He was trying to force his way in...into a building that was clearly too far gone already. If he went inside...

"Ethan!" she screamed as he rammed the door once more. He ignored her, determined to try and help Dr. Kessler.

Suddenly her feet were moving, carrying her to the burning building. The door gave way. Ethan was inside. Her heart bumped mercilessly against her ribcage.

"Ethan!"

She couldn't see anything through the thick smoke billowing from the open door.

"Ethan!" she screamed again. She had to do something. What if he'd been overcome by the smoke? What if she couldn't find him before it was too late? She had to go inside. She couldn't wait any longer.

Just as she started into the building, he burst out the door, Dr. Kessler thrown across one wide shoulder.

"Is he alive?" She helped Ethan lower him to the ground. They needed him alive. She shook herself. What was she thinking? She didn't want him to die whether he could help her or not.

"Barely. Go inside and call 911!"

Ethan's face and clothes were blackened by the smoke. He was breathing hard, coughing even harder. A chunk of ice formed in her stomach. He probably needed emergency medical care himself.

She was on her feet and running back toward the house before she realized she'd even moved. Help. She had to call for help.

Halfway to the house another explosion made the ground beneath her feet tremble. A force she couldn't see carried her backwards and flung her to the ground.

Ethan's face floated before her eyes.

She tried to speak but blackness swallowed her.

# Chapter Six

"She'll be fine. She's just a little shaken."

"Good." Relief flooded Ethan, making his knees weak. "Thanks for meeting me here, Doc."

Dr. Kyle Pendelton smiled and offered his hand. "I didn't mind at all. You're sure you're all right?"

"I'm good." A little rattled, Ethan didn't add.

He clasped the doc's hand and gave it a hearty shake. "Victoria will appreciate your going out of your way like this." Though he would certainly have done so if necessary, Ethan was glad he hadn't had to take Jennifer to a hospital. He didn't want to have to answer the questions that would no doubt have come up. Crane would likely have someone monitoring the hospitals if he suspected that she was still alive, and he clearly did.

Ethan hated like hell that he hadn't been able to do anything for Kessler. But he'd been pretty much a goner when Ethan emerged from the burning lab with him. Minutes later he'd been dead.

Ethan had called Dr. Pendelton on his cell phone as he'd driven like a bat out of hell from Kessler's place. He'd then reported the explosions to the 911 operator, which would create problems later, but he couldn't not report it. He'd worry about answering any questions the authorities had later. Victoria would keep them off his back until this case was under control.

Dr. Pendelton, medical bag in hand, paused at the door. "Actually it was closer for me to come here than to try and meet you across town at the hospital." He glanced around the rustic cabin once more before leaving. "Max has a great place here."

Ethan forced a smile. "I'll tell him you said so."

"Call me anytime."

"Will do."

Ethan watched Pendelton go, then closed and locked the door. The doc, as he was known to the investigators at the agency, had a small private practice. He'd been out of the business of practicing big medicine ever since his wife and child were kidnapped and murdered. Nowadays, he dropped everything and jumped anytime the agency called him. The Colby Agency had solved the case for him when the police couldn't. It hadn't brought his wife and daughter back, but it had given Pendelton closure and a great deal of comfort to know the bastard who destroyed his young family was behind bars serving consecutive life sentences.

Ethan glanced up the stairs, his thoughts returning to the woman resting quietly in Max's bed. His gut tightened. She'd almost been killed today because he'd sent her back to the house to make that call. He couldn't have known there would be a bomb in the house, too, but it was his fault just the same. She was under his protection. Maybe none of it would have happened,

Kessler might even still be alive, if Ethan had just believed her in the beginning. But he'd wanted proof. Crane obviously had had his men watching Kessler's place. With all three of them there, it had been the perfect opportunity to take them all out at once. Ethan wondered what had gone wrong. Why hadn't the house and lab blown simultaneously? Why the delay? Someone's obvious mistake was all that had saved their lives.

Now they were back at square one. With the lab destroyed, he still didn't have anything he could point to in order to prove his case to the authorities, but now he knew the truth. And, unfortunately for David Crane, that was all Ethan needed. He would not rest until he'd brought the man down. No matter what had happened in the past, Crane was his and he intended to stop him.

One way or another.

Ethan clenched his jaw. The idea that Crane had taken advantage of Jennifer, had tried to kill her, made Ethan see red. She was so young…so innocent of the evil men like Crane could do. She couldn't have imagined what he held in store for her. The idea of her with him was even more disturbing to Ethan.

Before he realized what he was doing, he was climbing the stairs two at a time. He needed to see for himself that she was resting comfortably. He was responsible for this. He should have believed her from the beginning.

She lay in the middle of the wide bed, the covers snuggled up around her, her eyes closed. Her long blond hair fanned out over the royal blue sheets. A familiar ache started deep inside him. He cursed himself for allowing it. She was all but a kid, whether she wanted to admit it or not. He should just go back downstairs and not risk disturbing her right now. He would rouse her every hour or so per the doc's instructions, he reminded himself as he backed down a step. But not now. Her eyes opened as if she'd sensed his presence.

"I'm awake," she said, her voice a little shaky.

He swallowed hard. He was just so damned glad she was okay. She'd taken a hell of a blow. It was a miracle she wasn't...

Ethan shook off the thought. "I didn't mean to disturb you. Is there anything I can get for you?"

She pushed up to a sitting position, grimacing as she did.

"Don't try to get up." He was across the room and at her side before she could move another muscle. "The doc said you should rest."

"We need a plan," she informed him, completely ignoring what he'd said. "We're running out of time. We have to stop David before he uses that drug on anyone."

Ethan placed his hands on her slender shoulders. "Don't worry, I'll stop him. All you have to do is rest." The feel of her skin beneath his palms surged through him like a shockwave. He hadn't realized until that moment that she didn't appear to have any clothes on. His mouth went sand-dry.

"Would you mind handing me that T-shirt?" Holding the covers to her chest with one hand, she pointed to the chair next to the bed.

"Sure." Ethan reached for the shirt. He should have

realized Pendelton would need to see her abdomen and back considering the brunt of the impact. He passed the shirt to her, purposely keeping his gaze turned away.

She released the cover long enough to pull the shirt over her head. He didn't look, but whether it was real or imagined, from the corner of his eye he caught just a glimpse of one breast. The small, firm globe tilted upward as if begging for attention. Every muscle in his body tensed. He had to get focused here. She was far too young for him, not to mention being his client.

"Since Kessler's evidence was destroyed, I don't see any other recourse. I'm going to have to confront David. I'm senior vice president, company security will have to listen to me," she announced.

She was climbing out of the bed. Ethan stopped her, clasping her arms and gently forcing her to sit back down. "How do you propose to do that?" She never ceased to amaze him, but this wasn't rational.

"I'll just walk in there and tell them what Kessler said. Having you on my side and the fact that Kessler is dead should prove something."

"Jenn," he said softly as he sat down on the side of the bed. She wasn't thinking straight. "If it had been that easy you wouldn't have needed me in the first place. Crane will have you killed."

"But you'll protect me." She looked up at Ethan with those big blue eyes. He couldn't have missed the respect there. He appreciated that, but it was the other thing he saw that bothered him. The same attraction he felt was mirrored there.

"Yes," he agreed, his voice tight. "I will. But first,

we have to be able to prove you are who you say you are.''

Realization dawned like a neon sign on a moonless night. She'd forgotten all about the other woman living her life at the moment.

''Oh, God. How will I ever be able to do that? She looks exactly like me. And, obviously, everyone at the lab has accepted her. The whole world thinks she's me.''

''We need her prints,'' Ethan said, considering the options.

''And her DNA,'' Jenn put in quickly, excitement building in her voice.

''But that won't prove anything without a comparison. We need several things.''

She pulled her knees up to her chest and looked at him with new hope in her eyes. ''Whatever we need we have to find a way to get it.''

Ethan tried not to notice the air of innocent vulnerability she radiated. ''In addition to her prints and DNA, we need yours.''

''No problem. I'll be happy to provide whatever is necessary.''

''And we need two comparisons.''

She frowned the tiniest bit. ''A DNA sample from my father?''

''That's one possibility. What we really need is something that would show your prints and, if we're really lucky, a DNA sequence from before. Something official with the name Jennifer Ballard on it.''

She bit her bottom lip with her pretty white teeth.

Ethan had to look away. The crazy need to soothe the sweet flesh she was tormenting was nearly overwhelming.

Her eyes suddenly lit up. "The security files at BalPhar will have my prints." Her expression drooped. "If David hasn't already changed all that."

"He probably wouldn't bother to change anything but the most recent files. Anything in storage or retired likely would be intact."

"That's it!" She was up on her knees right next to him now. "The retired files."

He grasped her shoulders again; even through the T-shirt her skin singed his palms. "You need to take it easy."

She grabbed his shoulders, the move sending a kind of quake rumbling through him. "Listen to me," she insisted. "Four years ago I participated in a study where they used DNA sequencing. It'll be there. David wouldn't know to change it. It was conducted before he came to BalPhar."

"Jenn," Ethan urged. He tried to ease her back down into a sitting position, but she resisted. "None of that matters right now. Right now you need to rest. I'll figure out something. I promise."

She looked at him as if trying to read what he was thinking. "Jenn," he warned. "You—" *have to stop looking at me that way,* he meant to say, but he lost his train of thought as his gaze moved of its own accord over her sweet face. Her right cheek was bruised and scraped just a little. He'd tried not to look at her this way, he'd known it wouldn't be a good idea. But it was too late now, he'd looked and he couldn't stop. Her cute little nose…those lush lips. Lips that looked entirely too kissable. The long, slender column of her creamy throat. His mind immediately produced the image of touching her there. His body reacted.

She leaned forward, blond silk caressing his hands where he still held her, his arms as she leaned closer still. His breath caught as her lips pressed against his. Desire erupted inside him like the mushroom cloud of a nuclear blast. His fingers tightened on her. The need to pull her closer, to take that sweet mouth was palpable, but he resisted and held her away when she would have wriggled closer.

"Jenn," he murmured, her mouth still against his, kissing him with a naïvetè that flooded him with protective feelings. This couldn't happen. He couldn't allow it. He should push her away, but his arms wouldn't make the necessary additional movement.

She drew back.

The tension coiling inside him relaxed just a fraction.

"Why won't you kiss me back?" She searched his eyes, looking for what he couldn't allow her to see.

He blinked all emotion from his eyes. "It's against the rules," he said tautly. "You're my client. Getting involved would be wrong for more than one reason."

"There's more to it than just that," she countered sagely.

She tensed beneath his touch. Belatedly, he drew his hands away. "You're just—"

"Don't even think about calling me a little girl

again," she threatened. "I'm not a little girl. I'm a woman."

There was a great deal of truth to her assertion, but still, she was far too young for a jaded guy like him. Though a dozen years spanned between them, this was about a great deal more than age.

He stood, determined to put some distance between them. "That may be, but that's beside the point. It's against the rules," he repeated.

She scrambled off the bed. He tried not to look at the length of toned legs revealed by the thigh-length T-shirt and her sudden move.

"Well, let me tell you something about the rules, *Mr. Delaney,*" she said fiercely. She advanced on him and he took a step back. "In the last week I've been dumped at the altar, ordered executed by the man I was supposed to marry, shot at and now almost blown up." She braced her hands on her hips and took another step in his direction. "Not to mention that some other woman I've never seen before has taken over my *life.* Everything is out of my control!"

Ethan held up his hands, hoping to stop her forward advancement. "You're right. You've been through hell. And in—" his voice faltered when she stopped right in front of him "—in situations like this, a person sometimes gets confused. You're just feeling the need to prove you're still alive, still desirable. Believe me, it has nothing to do with me. You'd only regret it afterward. It'll pass."

She lifted a skeptical eyebrow. "I'm not confused," she argued. "I know exactly what's on my mind. I've lost control of my whole world, almost been killed and may be killed yet. My entire life has been sheltered from this kind of thing. Absolute control, that's all I know.'' She threw up her hands in exasperation. ''And now it's all been taken away from me.''

''I know it's difficult,'' he reasoned, ''but—''

''You don't get it,'' she cut him off. ''The only thing I have any control left over at all is what *I* do right here and now.'' She hitched a thumb at her chest. ''Just me.''

Ethan braced himself. He had a bad feeling about this.

''And I absolutely do not intend to die a virgin. So get over yourself, Delaney, I'm over twenty-one and I know what I want. And right now, it's you.''

JENN WANTED to die.

How could she have done anything so utterly stupid?

She'd demanded that Ethan Delaney have sex with her. A flush heated her cheeks. Obviously that blast had rattled her brains worse than even the doctor had realized.

Going downstairs was out of the question. She retraced her steps across the room. She'd just stay up here and starve. No way was she facing him again. The afternoon had faded into night and nothing was resolved.

Her whole life was out of control.

Uncle Russ was dead.

Dr. Kessler was dead.

Was her father safe? Was he even still alive?

Worry settled over her like a wet blanket. She had to

find a way to prove she was Jennifer Ballard. She had to bring David down. The bastard.

She stomped her foot and then stamped back to the other side of the room. It was the only way she could get back to her father. Had his condition deteriorated even more? Would she be too late?

Tears burned her eyes. She didn't want to cry. She wanted to do something.

She should talk to Ethan.

She huffed. Yeah, right. Talking with him was out of the question. She crossed her arms and made a face at her reflection in the mirror. Since when had she started calling him Ethan? He was Delaney to her. *Investigator* Delaney. Nothing else.

How on earth could she have said what she said to him?

Growling with frustration, she spun around and paced in the other direction. She'd never behaved in such a manner. She'd barely allowed David to kiss her and he'd been her fiancè! She'd wanted to remain a virgin until her wedding night. Fat lot of good it would do her now. She was probably going to die just like Russ, like Kessler.

And she'd never know what it was like to share her body with a man she cared about. To make love.

What a joke. She belonged in a lab peering through a microscope. That was her world, not this insanity. And she certainly didn't give one hoot about Ethan Delaney. He was just…just…

"Nobody," she muttered.

A little voice deep inside her objected, but she ignored it. She barely knew the man. So what if he'd saved her life twice in the last twenty-four hours? It was his job. He was no hero, just hired help.

Another objection rang out loud and clear in her head.

"Shut up," she hissed.

She needed a distraction. And it definitely was not Delaney. She came up short as she spied the CD player on the bureau near the closet. Why hadn't she noticed that before? she thought as she headed toward it. She rolled her eyes. Easy, she'd been too busy being shot at and blown up to notice much...except the way he moved.

Jenn stilled, her fingers resting on the stack of CDs next to the player. There was something about the way he moved. Whether he was walking or scooping her up into those powerful arms. Something sexual. Predatory, yet alluring. After the second explosion, he'd knelt beside her, calling her name. She hadn't been able to hear him at first, but she'd watched his lips. At least an hour had passed before she could hear properly again, but she could feel. He'd moved his hands over every square inch of her, feeling for injuries of any sort, broken bones or what have you. He'd cradled her face in those big hands and promised her that everything would be fine.

Then, once he was convinced it was safe to move her, he'd lifted her against his chest. She'd settled there as if she were home. Her soft body had fitted perfectly against his hard, muscular one. And the way he'd smelled. She took a long, deep breath, closing her eyes to savor the memory. Even with the smell of smoke and soot clinging to his clothes and skin, there had been an underlying scent of pure male. An earthy, sensual essence that made her shiver. No man had ever held her like that. Even now warmth rushed through her at the memory.

Jenn shook her head and focused on flipping through the CDs. She had to do something to get her mind off her father and David Crane. And Ethan Delaney. She could think of only one thing that didn't involve her forbidden thoughts about Delaney—her one passion besides medical research, dancing.

Well, she considered, as she studied the titles on one CD in particular, it was a toss-up whether it was the dancing or the music. Whichever it was, when she wanted to lose herself, to put work out of her mind, she could turn on the music and let everything else slip away. She needed to work out her muscles anyway. They'd taken a beating today. A good workout and then another long, hot bath might lessen the coming soreness.

Good old Max had himself a pretty cool music selection of CDs. She put on one of her favorites, cranked up the volume and closed her eyes to soak up the vibes. In seconds her body was moving to the slow, rhythmic beat. Without opening her eyes, she tied the oversize T-shirt at her waist, not once breaking the fluid rhythm she felt all the way to her marrow. At twelve, she'd fancied professional dancing in her future. She'd secretly spent every spare moment watching every music video she could find with real dancers showcased.

Nothing came close to making her feel this free, this

exhilarated. Well, except maybe developing a new life-saving drug.

She'd taken dance classes as a little girl—ballet, tap, jazz—and she'd loved them all. But at seven, when her mother died, all that had changed. Her father had taken her into his world. And she'd grown to love it. She was at home there, felt safe. Still, the music stayed in her blood.

But David Crane had taken all that away from her. Made her familiar world a frightening place. She missed a step, but forced herself to relax and float with the melody, with the lyrics.

That was the worst travesty of all. He'd shattered her trust. He hadn't hurt her as deeply as he could have because she'd never loved him the way she was sure she should have. Time would have brought the depth to her feelings, she'd felt sure. Certainly she'd cared, but not enough, apparently. The hurt he'd wielded had been to her trust...to her concept of all that was right in the world.

Nothing would ever be the same again.

Nothing but the music.

Jenn forced all thought from her mind and moved with the angst-filled tenors drifting from the speakers.

She arched her back, flowing through a couple of feline moves, then spun around and sank to the floor in a flourish as the final notes played.

Her heart was pounding, but she felt more relaxed than she had in—

The sound of enthusiastic clapping jerked her head up.

*Delaney.*

Dammit. She felt color rise from her toes all the way to the roots of her hair. She shot to her feet and quickly turned off the CD player before the next selection began.

"What are you doing sneaking up on me like that?"

He shrugged, grinning like the Cheshire cat. "I didn't sneak up on you. You had the music on so loud you couldn't hear me. I called your name a couple of times."

She was reasonably sure she didn't believe that, but she was far too humiliated to argue. "What do you want?"

That grin dimmed a little, but the effect was breath-stealing. The smile it melted into was the most sensual thing she'd ever seen. And she hated it.

"I thought you might be hungry." That dark gaze roved down the length of her body, pausing where the T-shirt was knotted, revealing a tiny slice of her tummy. "I know I'm starved."

"I hope you're a better chef than you are an investigator." She jerked the knot loose, freeing the T-shirt, and dared him to argue her point. "After all, we still aren't any closer to solving this puzzle."

To her chagrin, he simply continued to measure her body. "I didn't know you liked to dance," he said, changing the subject.

"There's a lot about me you don't know." She marched up to him. "Excuse me," she snapped as she sidled past him.

"I'll just bet there is," he said smugly as she double-timed it down the stairs.

When she reached the bottom, she turned back and glared up at him as he descended more slowly. "I guess when you get older you lose all your mystery," she tossed at him, aiming low.

A challenging gaze locked with hers. He took a step down, then another, each move deliberately, intensely sensual. "Oh, I don't know, I think I'm still a mite mysterious. You'll probably be surprised to learn that I like to dance, too."

"Oh, really," she countered. She didn't believe him for one minute. He was making that up. If she'd said she liked to decorate cakes, he'd probably have said he did, too. He was obviously just making conversation, trying to get back on her good side. Well, he could forget it.

He'd had his chance and he'd blown it.

The only thing she wanted from him now was for him to do his job. The one for which she would eventually pay him.

He paused on the last tread, looking down at her with an intensity that unsettled her. She shivered inwardly. He was already nearly a foot taller than she. His position on the last step only made him tower over her even more.

"Really," he said softly.

The one word, combined with the intensity in his eyes made her sway on her feet. She grappled for the newel post.

"I'm especially good at dancing in the dark." He took the last step down, looked her over once more then said, in that same soft, sexy voice, "Maybe when you grow up I'll show you."

## Chapter Seven

"I know it goes against your nature," Ethan said the next morning. "But you're sure you'll sit right here in the car? You won't put the window down or get out for anything?"

She sighed loudly. "I told you this is not a car, it's an SUV. A seriously overpriced one. You probably got screwed when you bought it."

Ethan scrubbed a hand over his face. "Just answer the question. Will you stay put?" He glared at her as he waited for her answer.

She shrugged. "Sure, why wouldn't I?"

Ethan forced his gaze forward until he could regain control of his temper. She was driving him up the proverbial wall. Last night's little dance routine hadn't helped. She'd had him as horny as hell and damned near ready to take her up on her earlier offer.

"If any of Crane's men see you, they'll kill you," he told her in as calm a voice as he could marshal.

"Duh," she said grudgingly. "I'm not getting out of the vehicle, okay? I won't move unless it blows up like that house did or bursts into flames. And even then, assuming I live through the initial combustion, I'll survey the sidewalk before I get out.''

She was killing him. ''Don't use the .22 I gave you unless you're absolutely certain the person you're aiming it at represents a threat. This one *is* loaded.''

''Yeah, yeah,'' she griped. ''I pull one Barney Fife and you won't let me live it down.''

Ethan had to go now or he was going to wring her neck. Why hadn't Victoria warned him that she was such a pain in the butt? Maybe he shouldn't have cancelled that call to Melbourne after all. ''I'll be out of there as quickly as possible.'' He thrust his cell phone at her. ''Don't hesitate to call 911 or even to drive away if you feel your position has been compromised.''

''Like I'm really going to drive away without you,'' she said with a baleful look heavenward.

''Listen to me, Jenn,'' he growled.

''That's Dr. Ballard to you,'' she pointed out.

Deep breath. Stay calm. Don't kill her. *You'll lose your job.* ''I'm a big guy, I can take care of myself. Your only concern should be your personal safety. I don't need any one looking out for me.''

''Fine,'' she said flippantly. ''I understand.''

He hoped to hell she did. ''As soon as I have what I need, I'll be back.''

''What *we* need,'' she corrected.

''Yeah.'' Ethan climbed out of the SUV, locking the doors behind him. Why was he worried about her disappearing? He'd never get that lucky.

Jenn watched Ethan—Delaney, she amended—disappear into the restaurant. She banished the memory of the way he walked immediately. She would not dwell on anything about him. There was too much at stake. She'd had her little side trip to hysteriaville, now it was over. She was all business.

Speaking of business, this was the wackiest plan she'd ever heard of, but it might work. As much as she hated to admit it, *he* could probably make it work. One of his cohorts at the Colby Agency had tapped into the other Jennifer Ballard's personal computer planner and discovered that she had lunch plans with a business associate today—at this restaurant. Ethan would make sure he had the table next to hers and when she left he would take something she'd used during the meal. A fork would do, he'd said, but a glass would be much better.

Prints and DNA could definitely be lifted from the glass, the fork was iffy. Well, Jenn should have thought of that. But she hadn't.

Hotshot Delaney had masterminded the whole plan. Victoria Colby had someone meeting them at the cabin later to take the glass to a special lab that would analyze the data in the next twenty-four to forty-eight hours.

Then Jenn would have her proof and could publicly go after David and the woman. Finally it would be over and she could be with her father again. She felt sick with worry about him. But there was nothing she could do except wait.

An elegant car, David's Mercedes, pulled to the curb directly in front of the five-star restaurant. Jenn held her breath and instinctively slid lower in the seat. Though she was sitting four cars back and the windows were tinted, this would be the first time she'd been this close to the woman.

The door opened, but Jenn couldn't really see anything until the woman stood. Despite having braced herself, Jenn gasped. The woman looked so much like her, exactly like her. And she was wearing Jenn's clothes.

"My favorite Donna Karan suit," she muttered. *Bitch.*

Shoes too. God, the woman was a replica of her all the way down to her feet.

Jenn shivered. It was like having someone walk across her grave. And she wasn't even dead…yet.

If David had his way, she would be soon. Very soon.

ETHAN WATCHED the maître d' show the look-alike to her table. A man Ethan didn't recognize waited for her there. Smiling, the man stood while she was seated.

When the maître d' returned, Ethan would ask for the table next to hers and then the waiting game would begin. He could only hope that Jenn—Dr. Ballard—would be as good as her word.

This time.

SIXTY-ONE MINUTES later, Ethan left the restaurant with the look-alike's wineglass in his jacket pocket. Dr. Ballard was waiting for him in the Navigator, just as she'd promised she would be.

When he slid behind the wheel, he grinned at her expectant gaze. "Got it."

Her sigh of relief was audible.

"Hold the plastic bag open."

While she held the evidence bag open, he carefully removed the glass and then deposited it inside.

"Now all we have to do is take my prints and draw a blood sample and get the comparison—" she sighed, defeated "—from the BalPhar files," she added slowly.

"Don't worry," he felt compelled to assure her. "I'll figure out a way."

Jenn prayed he would.

But at the moment she couldn't conceive of a way either of them could break into BalPhar. It was far too secure. David had likely changed the security data to match the other woman. The woman he'd hired to pretend to be her. *His wife.*

Jenn forced her gaze straight ahead and banished thoughts of David Crane and his imposter wife from her mind. Instead, she thought about her father and all the wonderful times they'd shared. The discoveries they'd made together. The faraway lands they'd visited on research trips.

She would get her life back.

David Crane would not stop her.

Please, God, let her father still be alive when that happened.

ETHAN PARKED next to a white rental car. The guy Victoria had sent to collect the testing material had obviously arrived. Victoria hadn't mentioned a name. But Ethan knew the code phrase. If their visitor didn't, well then he might just end up buried behind Max's house.

Ethan almost smiled at that one. He was too tired to

work up sufficient compassion. The car could belong to someone lost in the woods. Yeah, right, he mused.

Max's cabin was about as lost as one could get.

No one would show up here by mistake.

Especially since Max'd had the cabin built here for that specific reason.

"We have company," Jenn said.

Ethan glanced at her. She looked tired, too. Until now, she hadn't spoken since they'd left the restaurant. He supposed she was worried about her father and what Crane was doing to her company. Ethan was worried about those things as well, but his weariness was caused more by her than anything else. She'd haunted him last night. Made him ache for her. Watching those slow, graceful moves had obliterated any hope he'd had left of keeping this fire building between them down to a manageable smolder. He'd be lucky to make it through another night without doing something totally stupid.

"It's the guy Victoria sent," he assured her, trying his level best to focus on the case.

"Are you positive?"

Ethan sighed. "I will be in a couple of minutes." He got out of the SUV, drawing his weapon as he went. "Stay behind me," he told her, for all the good it would do.

The realization that she still had the .22 brought him up short. He glanced over his shoulder. "And don't draw that weapon I gave you unless I'm already on the ground and bleeding."

She muttered something indistinguishable.

Ethan surveyed the small yard around the house, and

the treeline that bordered that. Nothing. There was no sound, discounting Jenn's tromping behind him. How could anyone who moved that gracefully to music make so much noise walking across a yard?

As Ethan mounted the porch steps, the front door swung inward. Instinctively he leveled his gun on the figure looming there. The man in the doorway reacted in kind.

"Delaney?"

"Nice weather we're having this summer," Ethan said.

A knowing look gleamed from the other man's eyes. "But not nearly as nice as last summer."

Ethan lowered his weapon. He offered the evidence bag he held in his left hand. "Mission accomplished."

"Good." The older man put his weapon away, took the evidence bag then extended his free hand. "I'm Lucas Camp, an old friend of Victoria's."

His gun tucked away, Ethan accepted the offered greeting. "I've heard of you," he said, his interest piqued.

Lucas cocked an eyebrow. "And I've definitely heard of you."

Jenn peeked past Ethan's arm. "This is Jennifer Ballard," Ethan said.

She stepped forward and shook Lucas's hand. "You can call me Jenn," she told him in a charming tone Ethan hadn't heard before.

He glowered at her when she flashed him the same sweet smile with which she'd just gifted their visitor.

Jenn watched Lucas Camp with extreme curiosity.

Not even the small scar beneath his right eye detracted from his good looks. He'd introduced himself as an old friend of Victoria Colby's. She couldn't help but wonder if the distinguished older man and the widow Colby had something going on. Man, she'd never spent so much time thinking about sex before. She glanced at Ethan—the bane of her existence. It had to be his fault. David had never disturbed her this way.

She doubted he ever would have.

Men like Ethan Delaney were a breed of their own.

She shivered. The kind of men daddies warned their little girls about.

*Little girl.*

Just the thought of him calling her that infuriated her all over again.

The conversation resumed at the dining table. She couldn't help but wonder if the chitchat was a move to help her relax before Lucas did what he'd come to do— obtain the necessary samples from her.

Lucas and Ethan discussed Ethan's time in the military. He'd been Special Forces and had specialized in retrieving hostages. As much as she hated to admit it, her respect for him grew just a tad. According to Lucas, Ethan had, without thought to his own safety, entered enemy territory numerous times to save lives. She supposed he was really good at his job, but that didn't make her like him any better. She could respect him, trust him even, without really liking him.

*Trust.* Did she really trust Ethan Delaney? Her father trusted Victoria Colby and she trusted her father. Jenn supposed she did trust Ethan on a certain level, but not beyond that. She wasn't sure she would ever trust anyone again on a truly personal level.

Lucas Camp opened what looked like a briefcase, ready to get down to business, obviously. ''Do you want me to take the samples or would you prefer that Ethan did the honors?'' he asked Jenn, drawing her back to the conversation.

Like she'd let Delaney get within a mile of her with a needle in his hand. ''You can do it.''

First he took her prints. It wasn't nearly as messy as she remembered. Lucas still hadn't said what line of work he was in, but judging by the discussion between Ethan and him, she wasn't sure she wanted to know. He sounded like one of those James Bond-type spies. She tamped down the urge to shiver.

Next he gently swabbed the interior of her mouth, then drew a small sample of blood. Ethan was conspicuously missing during the proceedings.

''They probably won't need the blood, but I'd rather get it while I'm here, just in case,'' he explained with a smile that was all charm and graciousness.

''How long before we have the results?'' Ethan asked, drawing Jenn's reluctant attention to him as he walked back into the room.

Why was it her body responded so to the mere sound of his voice? She didn't like that giddy little feeling it gave her. She wanted to keep pretending she didn't care.

''Forty-eight hours tops,'' Lucas told him. ''The Cessna is standing by to take me back to D.C. You can fax me the prints and the DNA sequence tonight. I'll be available all night.''

Prints? DNA sequence?

The BalPhar files.

"How do you plan to get those files out of BalPhar?" she demanded of Ethan who was suspiciously avoiding her gaze.

"Someone else is going to stay with you while I go in and retrieve them tonight."

Jenn stood, the legs of her chair scraping across the wood floor. "No way you're going in without me."

"It's too dangerous, *Dr. Ballard*," Ethan said firmly. "Simon Ruhl will keep you safe until I return. He's good at what he does. You'll be safe with him."

"And what if you're caught?" she demanded.

He held her gaze, his unwavering. He'd made up his mind. "Then Simon will take over the case. You'll be safe either way."

Lucas Camp watched the exchange with interest. Jenn used that to her advantage.

"Tell him, Lucas, that he's crazy. It's too dangerous."

"It's dangerous, that's true, but—"

Her hands went to her hips as her anger mounted to a new level. "The security is too tight. You'll never get in without a breach. Besides, I know right where the files are." There, she mused, let him top that.

"So," Ethan said tightly. "You'll draw me a map. I don't need you in there getting in my way."

Another blast of fury slammed into her. But a long-forgotten memory brought a smile to her face. "You're not going in," she told him flatly. "I am. And I won't even have to break in. I have access."

Ethan stood, towering over her, cranking up the intimidation, coming down hard with a fierce expression that far exceeded any other she'd seen from him. "Whatever access you had will have been altered for the *other* Dr. Ballard," he growled, the tone menacing.

Jenn shook her head, grinning from ear to ear. God, she was enjoying this. She had an ace up her sleeve and he didn't have a clue. "I have another ID."

"What?" Ethan demanded.

Lucas Camp just smiled, thoroughly enjoying the sparring.

"When I was still in college I liked to sneak into the lab after hours to work on a secret project I had going."

Ethan folded his arms determinedly and waited for her to give him something better than that.

"But security keeps a record of all the comings and goings. A record that my father reviewed every morning. So, I created a profile on a new maintenance employee." She waggled her eyebrows. "A fictitious one. I never deleted it. *I can get in.* No sweat."

"What kind of checks do they have?" Lucas asked.

"Palm and retina scans," Ethan grouched. "It's still too risky. I don't care about getting in through the front door. I'm happy to go in through the back. *Alone.* Especially since Simon is available now to help out."

"Tell him I'm right and he's wrong," Jenn said to Lucas Camp. "Why do it the hard way, right?"

Lucas inclined his head and raised an eyebrow at Ethan. "She's got a point."

Ethan swore. The scorching four-letter word startled her. He was madder than hell.

"Fine," he snapped. "We'll do it your way." He stared long and hard at her. "But remember, it wasn't my idea."

"Your objection is duly noted," she said saccharinely.

His stare turned to a glower, which he promptly shifted in Lucas's direction. "Thank you, too."

Lucas flared his hands. "I'm always happy to oblige." He picked up the briefcase containing the samples. "I'll be standing by for your fax."

Ethan walked outside with him. Jenn hadn't noticed the older man's slight limp until then. She wondered what had caused it. An accident of some sort, she supposed. He certainly looked fit and athletic enough. She chuckled. A skiing accident, maybe.

When Ethan returned those dark eyes were shooting daggers at her. "You'd better get some rest. We head out in seven hours."

She gave him her most exuberant smile. "I'll be ready."

AT MIDNIGHT Ethan stopped the SUV on the rise about a half mile from BalPhar's entrance gate. He didn't like this.

"You're sure you want to do this?" he asked one last time. They'd already been over this before they left the cabin. But he had to give her one more chance to back out.

"Positive." She beamed a smile at him.

She was almost lost in the darkness. They both wore black caps, black turtlenecks, black gloves, black cargo pants and boots. Ethan was taking no chances. If they had to make a hasty getaway, they were prepared. Flashlights, electronic security decoder, and whatever else he'd deemed necessary. Most of the items were in the backpack he would wear.

"All right. Let's do it."

Though the whole thing still didn't sit right with him, he exchanged seats with her so that she would be on the driver's side for the sake of any cameras they might encounter. When they reached the gate, she got out of the vehicle and placed her hand on the scanner inside a small booth that looked much like a hooded pay-phone setup. She leaned forward and held very still for the retina scan. Five seconds later, the gate opened to allow them entrance.

Three minutes after that they had entered the building. The caps were pulled down lower to shield as much of their faces as possible without obstructing vision as they skirted the areas with surveillance cameras.

Without speaking, Jenn led the way down to the file archives on basement level one. BalPhar had three levels underground, Ethan learned. Jenn explained in a whisper that the lower two levels were used for working with extremely contagious viruses or otherwise toxic chemicals.

Ethan continued to scan warily as Jenn located the right files. The thermal scanner he'd brought along showed no sign of life anywhere within one hundred yards of their location.

"Here's the security file from three years ago when I first became senior vice president."

Ethan placed the pages from the file he needed into an evidence bag and tucked it into the backpack. He handed the folder back to Jenn.

Fifteen minutes passed before she found the file that contained her DNA sequence from the four-year-old study. The one Crane couldn't possibly know about, she had assured Ethan. He placed the required pages in the plastic bag with her documented prints, then passed the folder and the remainder of its contents back to her.

He delayed her when she would have rushed to the elevator. "Take it slow," he warned, whispered. "We're this close—" he held his left thumb and forefinger only an inch apart "—to being out of here. We don't want to screw up now. Somewhere in this building there's night security. We can't risk running into one of them. Got me?"

She nodded.

A new kind of respect sprouted inside him right then and there. This little girl was a lot braver than he'd given her credit for. Which only made him want her more.

He sighed. She frowned, a question in her big blue eyes.

"Let's go." He released her arm.

Still looking confused, she turned and led the way back out of the building.

THE TELEPHONE buzzed softly.

David Crane roused from sleep and reached for it. He came instantly alert. A call this time of night could not be good.

"Yes."

"Mr. Crane, I apologize for waking you at this hour."

It was Graham, chief of night security at BalPhar.

"You did the right thing," David said, then cleared the sleep from his voice. "What's happened?"

"Sir, you said we should notify you directly if anything unusual occurred at the facility."

"Yes." David pushed to a sitting position, adrenaline rushing through him.

"A maintenance employee has entered the building," Graham explained. "I wouldn't have thought anything about it except that it's an employee I'm not familiar with. I pulled her file and it's several years old. It's been inactive for over three years."

A slow smile spread across David's face. "Is she still in the building?"

"Yes sir."

"I want you to put a tracking device on the vehicle she arrived in. Do it now. I don't want her to get away without it."

"But, sir, I could stop her now. She's in the basement. I can have four men down there in thirty seconds."

"No," David said sharply. So sharply the woman sleeping next to him moaned softly. "Do not, I repeat, do not approach her. I don't want an incident at the facility." Nor did he want anyone to see Jenn up close. It would only raise questions. "Do exactly as I instructed. If that vehicle gets off the grounds without a tracking device it'll be your job."

"Yes, sir."

David replaced the handset on the base. *Gotcha!* he mused. "You won't get away this time, darling," he muttered as he threw the covers back and climbed out of bed. He was still furious about yesterday's fiasco. If his men couldn't orchestrate a simple double bombing, then perhaps he needed to retire them. *Permanently.*

He'd have that bitch right where he wanted her by morning. Six feet under. He laughed at the notion. She'd made this harder than it should have been. And once he was certain she and her friend were out of the way, David would take care of the final loose end.

He entered Austin Ballard's bedroom as quietly as a church mouse. He flipped on the overhead light and walked straight to the bed and sat down next to the dying old man.

David roused him just to make sure he was still breathing. The old man groaned and opened his eyes. It took him a few moments to focus, then fear glittered in those faded blue depths.

"Soon," he warned. "Very soon you'll be out of your misery. And I'll have all that ever mattered to you."

Austin Ballard moaned pathetically, tears shone in his aged eyes. Despite his inability to lift his head from the pillow, he was very much aware of what was going on around him.

David patted his arm when he reached a feeble hand toward him. "Don't worry," he said with a menacing smile, "I'm taking care of her, too."

Back in his own room David made one final call before slipping back into bed. "You have them?"

The voice on the other end of the line responded affirmatively.

"Good. If they live to see another day, you won't."

# Chapter Eight

"That was too easy."

Ethan kept a close watch on the rearview mirror as they drove through North Aurora. He'd glimpsed headlights since they left the BalPhar compound. Someone had followed them. There was no other traffic, just the persistent pair of headlights far behind them. Dammit. He'd known something wasn't right from the moment they entered the building. It was just too easy. Instinctively he stepped a little harder on the accelerator.

Jenn jerked off her knit cap. In his periphery he saw all that silky blond hair fall around her shoulders. His fingers ached to touch it; instead, he gripped the steering wheel more tightly.

"We did it," she enthused.

"I'm not sure we got away as clean as you think."

"You are such a pessimist." She tossed the cap aside. "I told you the security ID I used was clean. Maybe tomorrow, when tonight's logs are reviewed, someone might question the sudden use of an inactive ID, but so what? We'll be long gone. We did it!" She relaxed back against the seat and sighed. "We have what we need now. By this time tomorrow I might have the proof necessary to get my life back.''

Ethan swore under his breath, his attention split between the winding road before him and the rearview mirror. ''Put that cap back on.'' The headlights were still back there. Way behind them, but there just the same. ''We've got company.''

Jenn whipped around in her seat. ''From BalPhar?''

''Yep.'' The lights were moving closer now.

She scrambled around the floorboard for the cap she'd discarded. ''Why do I need to put this back on? What good will it do?''

''We don't want our tail to see all that blond hair. Now put it back on.'' Eighty registered on the speedometer now and still they were gaining on him.

''Do we have to go this fast? This road has a lot of twists and turns.''

He doused the lights. ''I know.''

''Are you insane? You just turned off the headlights!''

He took the next curve a little faster than he would have preferred. His fingers tightened on the wheel. Adrenaline burned through his veins. ''Get that .22 out just in case you have to use it.'' Mercy, he hated to have her this close and armed, but she just might prove useful.

''Can't you outrun them without going too fast?'' Fear was thick in her voice. She rummaged for the .22 in the glove compartment. ''I've never tried to shoot anyone before. I think maybe you'd better come up with an alternative plan.''

Big surprise. Bracing himself for the inevitable, he floored the accelerator, picking up more speed. "I'm working on it."

Her only response was a gasp.

The woods and houses on either side of the road blurred into one dark mass as the Navigator shot forward like a ground rocket.

"Oh, God," she cried, "they're right behind us!"

"Tell me something I don't know," Ethan muttered.

A sharp crack rent the air. The passenger-side mirror shattered.

"What was that?" she shrieked.

Before he could respond, she'd unfastened her seatbelt and was climbing across the console in his direction.

"Stay down!" he roared.

The steering wheel jerked as the tires on the right side left the pavement briefly. He cut the wheel left, bouncing back onto the asphalt and still managing to gain speed. Thankfully she hovered low in the seat. If she would just stay there, he could concentrate on losing these bastards. A rear window crashed. Ethan's shoulders lifted in an instinctive move to protect the nape of his neck.

"They're shooting at us!" Jenn said suddenly as if realization had only just dawned. She flung herself onto the floorboard.

Dammit. He had to lose this tail.

"Get that seat belt back on," he barked.

Keeping her head down, she clambered into the seat and did as he instructed. Another shot pierced the windshield right between them. He couldn't return fire and drive. He wouldn't risk her making an attempt to return fire.

With no other alternative, Ethan slammed on the brakes and swerved violently to the left. The SUV skidded sideways then fishtailed, tires screeching and burning, the smell of rubber filling the air. Jenn clung to the seat, her feet braced against the dash, a long *o-h-h-h-h-h n-o-o-o-o* of absolute terror escaping her lips.

Ethan gunned the accelerator again, heading in the opposite direction. The engine roared as he zoomed past the silver SUV sliding sideways in the opposite lane. He couldn't be sure if these were the same guys who had shot at them earlier or not. The vehicle was definitely different.

"Are you trying to get us killed?" she screamed the moment inertia no longer pinned her to the seat. "Stop this car right now! You're driving like a maniac."

Ethan gritted his teeth and ignored her. The SUV was coming after them again, eating up the asphalt between them.

"Stop this instant and let me out! I'll take my chances on the ground!"

Sheer panic had her in its grip now. "Just hold on."

Suddenly the .22 was jammed into his right temple. "I said stop the damned car. I'm getting out of here before you kill us both."

There was no time to think or question the move. A fleeting glimpse of a side road up ahead came into view. There were no houses in the immediate vicinity. Two seconds later they were on top of the turn. He took it, simultaneously elbowing her arm upward. Tires squealed. The .22 fired, sending a tiny spear of steel through the SUV's roof before the weapon flew out of her hand and over the seat. Jenn screamed, creating a high-pitched cacophony of fear.

The Navigator jerked and bounced, sliding sideways as it cleared a path where one had not previously existed. The eerie sound of brush and tall grass whipping against metal filled the thick silence inside the vehicle. Then, with a force that flung them both forward, the vehicle came to an instant, bone-jarring halt. The engine died with a hissing sound.

For three beats Ethan couldn't move, his face buried in a smothering pillow. The airbags deflated as rapidly as they had inflated.

"Run!" he roared at his passenger.

She looked dazed but he saw no sign of injury.

"Run, dammit!" He snagged the backpack from the back seat and barreled out of the Navigator.

Jenn was frozen. She couldn't move. Her head was spinning. Her ears were ringing. Ethan was shouting at her. Suddenly her door burst open and he manacled her wrist in one powerful hand. He hauled her out of the car and started running.

"Wait," she begged, her knees buckling beneath her.

Her stomach quaked with fear, her hands were icy. She couldn't do this. Expelling the contents of her stomach appeared imminent. God, she'd shot a hole through the roof of his car! He was still dragging her forward.

The sound of car doors slamming somewhere behind them sent ice plunging through her veins. Fainting became a distinct possibility. Surely someone along this stretch of road would wake up and call the police.

No one would help them, she realized with sudden clarity.

It was over.

*They were dead.*

Jenn wilted, her legs going rubbery again.

"Run, dammit!" Ethan yelled as he dragged her forward through the waist-deep underbrush.

A bullet whizzed right past her left ear and lodged in a nearby tree.

She jerked with recognition. Head still spinning and gasping for breath, Jenn needed no additional prompting. She ran like hell.

Ethan's hand was clamped around her wrist. It was so dark she could scarcely make out the shape of trees as they barreled past them. Half stumbling, half running she stayed hot on Ethan's heels. If he could see where he was going that was great; she couldn't see a thing. Even his large frame seemed lost in the darkness. She prayed hers was as well. Thank God they were dressed completely in black.

The pounding of footsteps and the rush of bodies through undergrowth exploded some thirty or forty yards behind them. The occasional shot pierced the thick gloom, smacking the ground or a tree entirely too close for comfort.

Ethan pushed forward, zigzagging to avoid being an easy target, she imagined. She realized then that the reason no one was going to wake up and call the police was because their pursuers were using sound suppressors. No one would hear a single gunshot.

Ethan's pace never slowed. He ran hard, tugging her along behind him.

Suddenly he altered his course, veering left. Another shot whistled past several feet to their right. Her lungs burned, ached for more oxygen. But she couldn't slow down, she had to run. She could hear the men crashing relentlessly through the thick brush behind them. Suddenly, incredibly they broke from the trees and bushes.

Ethan stopped abruptly. Jenn slammed into his broad back. His hand gripped her wrist even tighter.

"What—"

"Can you swim?"

The instant her brain assimilated his question her ears relayed the analysis of the unfamiliar new roar in the darkness.

*Water.*

A shiny, curving black snake of swiftly moving water lay in their path.

In that same instant she realized his intention.

"I can't—" A bullet hissed by, splashed into the murky water.

"Jump!"

He propelled his body forward, a ruthless grip on her wrist, leaving her no choice.

The water closed around her, blinding her, filling her mouth before she had the good sense to close it, surging up her nose and choking off any hope of taking a breath. She kicked and flailed her arms in an attempt to swim. Of course, she couldn't. She'd been terrified of water since she was a small child. Avoided it at all costs, except for bathing, and even then, one hand always gripped the side of the tub.

She sank lower. Deeper into the darkness. And surrendered to the inevitable. She was going to die.

A huge black shape was suddenly lunging toward her. She watched with morbid fascination. It was over, why fight it? Something suddenly grabbed her hand, viciously, ruthlessly yanking her upward.

Her face broke the surface of the water.

She gasped for air. Coughed, sputtered, expelling as much water as possible to make room for air.

She struggled violently to keep her mouth and nose above the surface, but she sank like a rock.

Another jerk on her wrist. Ethan was there…dragging her up and then down the river, or at least she thought they were moving. Her head bobbed upward. She gulped a mouthful of air. Just as she went under again, she heard the splashing pings of bullets hitting the water.

Ethan's dark form lunged for her again, this time hauling her ruthlessly to the surface with one arm banded around her waist.

"All you have to do is be still," he ordered, his voice something between a roar and a whisper. "I'll keep you afloat if you don't drown me first."

She was plastered against him. Her chest flat against his. Fear streaked through her as she felt herself sinking once more. Instinctively she wrapped her legs around the closest solid form—Ethan. In a blind panic, her arms curled around his neck in a last-ditch effort to stay afloat.

"Relax," he growled, the last syllable more of a gurgle as his own head went down.

She felt him trying to pry her loose, but she wasn't letting go, not as long as she was alive, anyway.

They both sank as if they had a bag of rocks attached to their waists.

Within the minute they broke the surface again.

No thanks to her.

She gasped, dragging air into her starved lungs.

"Turn loose," he growled savagely. "You're going to drown us both."

His powerful legs were kicking, keeping them afloat.

"Turn me loose!" he croaked.

She couldn't…wouldn't.

When they started to sink again, he grabbed her arms and pulled them loose from his neck with a strength that startled her. He twisted free of her legs and lunged ahead. She sank like a stone. Her heart pounded. He was leaving her.

Suddenly he was there again.

He whipped her around and spooned her body against his, then struggled back to the surface.

Air rushed into her lungs.

"Just relax. Don't move a muscle or I'll drown you myself."

Considering his savage tone, she didn't doubt he would do just that.

She struggled to catch her breath. She could hear the men's voices on the bank they'd left behind, but they were distant. How had they moved so far? Only then did she realize how very fast the water was flowing.

A beam of light suddenly streaked across the water.

"Damn." Ethan stroked harder, propelling them toward the bank on the other side of the river. "Keep your head down so they can't see your face."

She turned her face toward his body and away from the light flitting across the surface of the water, searching for them. If they were just quiet enough—fast enough—they'd make it to the other side without being spotted.

"Don't struggle," he warned, his lips brushing her forehead. "Just relax against me. I'm a good enough swimmer to get us both to the other side."

She could feel his powerful legs moving behind her. Closing her eyes, she finally did relax. Her heart rate slowed. Her respiration followed suit.

"Almost there," he muttered harshly.

For the first time since this adventure had begun, she heard fatigue in his voice. She prayed he wouldn't give out before they reached dry land. The men chasing them had given up finding them on foot and were now driving their silver SUV along the riverbank, shining the light over the water.

Another abrupt reality crashed into Jenn's skull. They'd wrecked Ethan's SUV and had no way out of here. Other than walking—running, she amended.

"We wrecked the car," she murmured, too weary, too cold to inject any real inflection into the words.

His one-armed stroke never slackened. "It's not a car," he said, breathless. "Remember?"

She smiled, in spite of their dire circumstances.

Suddenly he was standing, hauling her limp body up with him. "We've got to keep moving. We don't want them to catch up."

She forced her feet to move. Like she had any choice. He was practically pulling her arm out of its socket. What else could she do but follow? How could he still have this much energy? He ran like the Energizer Bunny…as if they hadn't already run for what felt like forever. As if he hadn't swum the width of the swiftly flowing river with her dead weight in tow.

She shivered uncontrollably at that last thought.

"Wait." Jenn stumbled, fell to her knees.

Ethan skidded to a stop. He dragged her back to her feet. "We can't stop."

"I have…to catch…my breath," she argued weakly, slumping against him. She felt suddenly cold. It was the middle of July, for goodness sake, but she was cold just the same. Freezing, actually. She trembled again.

Before Jenn could fathom his intent, he'd braced his shoulder at her waist and lifted her off her feet.

"What…what are you doing?" she demanded feebly.

"Keeping us alive."

ETHAN DEPOSITED his cargo onto the steps of the tiny back stoop of a small cottage. He'd gone about as far as he could. He was spent.

He straightened, grimacing with the effort. It wasn't that she was heavy, definitely not. He doubted she weighed a hundred pounds soaking wet, and she was definitely soaking wet. As was he.

"Where are we?" she mumbled, making a valiant effort to struggle to her feet.

"I'm not sure." He peered through the window at the back door looking for signs of life. He tried the knob. To his surprise it turned. "Sit tight," he told her. He could only hope that she was too damned tired to do otherwise.

Inside he quickly retrieved his night vision goggles from the backpack, and dumped the rest of the contents onto the countertop to see that all was secure. He then surveyed each room. Though definitely lived in, the place was uninhabited at the moment. He wondered if it was a weekend cottage.

He hoped like hell the residents were at the very least gone for the night. There wasn't a telephone, which meant they would have to wait until morning to find a phone to call for a replacement vehicle, since the cellular phone he'd had in his jacket hadn't survived the river.

Jenn was still leaning against the railing when he slipped out the back door once more. The relief he felt made him weak. He'd halfway expected to find her gone. "We can crash here for a while. At least as long as we don't have any company."

She looked too tired to care one way or the other. "Great. I don't think I could survive another confrontation tonight."

Once inside, she turned to Ethan, "It's awfully dark in here."

"We can't turn on any lights. It's too risky. They may still be looking for us."

She shivered. He didn't actually see her, but she was standing so close he felt it.

"Cold?"

She nodded vigorously.

"There's a dryer. Take your clothes off and I'll dry them for you."

He sensed her hesitation. "I need something else to put on," she said timidly.

A grin tugged at Ethan's mouth. Where was the little flirt dressed in nothing but a towel who'd teased him?

"Don't worry, I can't see a thing," he assured her. She didn't have to know about the night vision. Not that he would use it to play Peeping Tom.

"Let me find a towel or blanket or something."

"Wait here, I'll get you something." It was the least he could do. He did have the night vision at his disposal after all.

He found a lightweight blanket for her and a towel for himself without going very far. She accepted the blanket, her hand shaking. He could just imagine how tonight had affected her. She'd pretended to be so brave when they entered the BalPhar facility. It wasn't until things had shifted into warp speed and the bullets had started flying that she'd lost control. He had to hand it to her, she was a trouper.

For a little girl, he reminded himself.

They both began to strip right there in the pitch-dark kitchen. He tried, but failed, to ignore the sounds of her undressing. The black sneakers thumped to the floor. The wet slap of socks landing next. The unmistakable sound of a zipper being lowered. The scrub of damp cargo pants sliding down shapely legs.

Ethan shook himself. Slow down, man, he warned his hardening body. She was a kid. Too young for him. Too innocent for him. And far too…

He groaned. She was a virgin.

She was definitely all wrong for him.

Even if she weren't a client.

"Is something wrong?"

She was standing right next to him and he was still only half-undressed. In his distraction, he'd allowed her to sneak up on him. *Get a grip, Delaney.* This wasn't the first naked female he'd been in a dark room with.

He lifted a skeptical brow; it probably was the first naked virgin.

He flexed his right arm, refocusing his considerable attention on the ache. He'd really worked it over swimming against that current. Not to mention hitting the motel-room floor and body-slamming the door to Kessler's lab.

She touched him. A soft hand on his naked shoulder. Heat shot through him, pooling in his groin.

"Are you okay?" she asked, her voice tentative.

"Yeah. I'm good." He shifted away from her touch. "You?"

"Fine." She sighed softly. "Thanks to you."

Oh, boy. Just what he *didn't* need. A misguided sense of gratitude popping up between them. And things were definitely *up*. Way up.

"I haven't finished…" He gestured vaguely to his partially clad body as if she could see.

"Well," she said, a smile in her voice. "Like you said, it's not as if either of us can see."

"Right," he agreed wryly.

He kicked off his sneakers, peeled off the socks, then slowly, carefully lowered the zipper of his pants. She'd made the process risky at best.

A sharply indrawn breath slowed his movements. He hesitated, his pants halfway to his knees. "I can go in the other room if you'd prefer."

"No," she squeaked. "I can't see a thing. I'm fine."

She shifted. He heard the rustle of the blanket against her bare skin. Ethan scrubbed a hand over his face and drew in a harsh breath of his own. She didn't have to see, apparently, she only had to be in the room.

"Go ahead," she urged when his hesitation dragged on.

Raw desire pumping through his tense body, he shucked the pants, then the briefs. He wrapped the towel around his waist and wondered what the hell they would do now. Or, if he didn't lose his mind altogether, what they wouldn't do.

"You should probably try to get some sleep." He gathered their wet clothes. "I'll keep watch."

"You don't need any sleep?" Whether she realized it or not, she stood between him and the dryer, which was on the other side of the room.

"I'll catch the forty winks I need." He skirted wide around her position. But still, every part of him reacted to the idea of her standing there in nothing but a thin blanket. "I learned to catch shut-eye in three-minute increments during my military days."

"Oh."

He opened the dryer door. The light that spilled across the floor was almost startling. It reached across the room and silhouetted her bare feet. The glow drifted upward, wrapping around her delicate ankles and toned calves. She stepped closer, unwittingly offering more of her legs in the light.

He tossed the clothes inside the dryer and slammed the door shut. After twisting the timer to start the machine, he said. "All done here." His hand closed over her elbow and she gasped again. He tried not to notice the feel of her skin beneath his fingers. He guided her down the hall and into the living room. All he had to do was get through this night. "You can have the couch. I'll take a chair."

The tension only got thicker…even with several feet of hardwood floor and a small coffee table between them. Every breath she took, every move she made, only added to his discomfort. He shifted first one way then another, but relief was not forthcoming.

A cold shower was the only possible solution, but he couldn't let down his guard long enough for that.

He'd just have to suffer.

Then she said the last thing he wanted to hear.

"Could we share the couch?" She made a sound, not quite a sigh but definitely on that order. "I'd feel safer with you over here."

Ethan rubbed a hand over his unshaven chin. "Yeah. Sure." He'd always been a glutton for punishment.

He stood. Adjusted his towel. It was a damn good

thing she couldn't see...or she might change her mind about sharing the couch.

The moment he sat down, she snuggled up next to him. "I'm sorry. I'm usually not this childish, but I don't like the dark. I always keep a light on."

With all they'd been through in the last forty-eight hours, the dark was the least of their worries.

"Thank you for saving my life again," she murmured. Her soft cheek felt like satin against his forearm.

"No problem," he muttered, annoyed with himself. She didn't have the first clue what she was doing to him. He wanted to kick himself for losing all signs of objectivity. This wasn't his style at all.

"Good night, Ethan."

"Good night, Dr. Ballard." Though he could see nothing good in store.

"You can call me Jenn," she whispered, pressing even closer. "Any man who's seen me naked, even in the dark, should be able to call me Jenn."

Ethan closed his eyes and dropped his head back onto the sofa. Just what he needed. A reminder that she was practically naked sitting right there next to him. If there was any justice in the universe she would go to sleep right now.

And he'd thought he'd escaped certain death by eluding the bad guys.

How could he have known that she was planning to kill him softly...all night long?

## Chapter Nine

Jenn awoke with a start. Her body ached, more from the sudden loss of skin-to-skin contact than from the night's adventures.

It was still dark. The room was pitch-black. The space next to her was warm, but there was no Ethan. Her heart fluttered into a faster rhythm.

A creak echoed somewhere in the enveloping darkness.

Someone was moving around inside the house.

Ethan?

For one trauma-filled instant Jenn couldn't move... couldn't scream.

Where was Ethan?

Had David's men found them?

No!

If he found her...

She bolted from the couch, blanket clutched around her shoulders. She ran, slipping on the hardwood floor as she went. She had to find Ethan. What if they'd hurt him already...killed him? She shuddered.

A gun? She needed a gun. Where was the backpack?

Cold, bony fingers of fear clutched at her heart as scenario after scenario flashed through her mind like a video on Fast Forward. The blood on her wedding gown…Uncle Russ dead on the floor. The lab exploding…the house…

An up-close and too-personal encounter with a doorframe almost knocked her flat on her back. She swore hotly, that scorching four-letter word she'd heard Ethan use when she'd insisted on going with him to BalPhar.

They'd barely escaped.

Had they been found now? They should have kept running, but she'd been so tired.

Too tired to go any farther.

That was likely why Ethan had opted to hide out here. *Ethan.*

She had to find Ethan. Had to escape.

Stumbling more than running now and rubbing her forehead where she'd been kissed by the doorframe, she surged forward into the long hall that split the cottage right down the middle. She considered calling his name, but if David's men were here she'd only give her position away.

If she allowed them to catch her she'd be no help to Ethan or her father.

She'd be dead.

Something large and very much like granite abruptly halted her forward movement. The hard, unyielding surface blended with the darkness. She frowned, squinting to see, instinctively drawing back. There was movement…reaching upward…another soft sound of something being moved.

Powerful arms went around her as enlightenment dawned. She'd slammed into a rock-solid body.

If it was Ethan, why didn't he say something?

She started to scream, but a hard mouth closed over hers, muffling the sound. She struggled to get away for another second, then recognition flared. Firm, full lips.

Ethan.

The smell of river water and that unique scent that was purely Ethan filled her nostrils.

Heat burst in her middle, melting her muscles, dissolving her bones. She sagged against that awesome torso. His mouth was warm and wonderful and extremely skilled. Almost punishing at first, the kiss had softened, grown tender. She'd never been kissed like this.

Never, ever before.

Then he stopped.

A whimper escaped her lips.

"They're outside," he whispered against her ear. "Two houses down."

Unadulterated fear surged through her, obliterating the warmth and the dreamy sensation that had enveloped her beneath his sensual assault. Instinctively he tightened his hold, those strong arms all that stood between her and slumping into a quivering mass on the floor.

"We have to move. *Now.*"

She nodded her understanding.

Her fingers clenched in his jacket. Only then did she realize that he was dressed. She opened her mouth to ask where her clothes were and he pressed a finger to her lips as accurately as if he could see in the thick blackness that cloaked them.

"Follow me. Be very, very quiet."

She nodded once more, the brush of his lips against the shell of her ear sending a shiver across her skin.

Holding her hand firmly, with his free hand he reached up again. She peered through the darkness, willing her eyes to see. He appeared to move something. A cap? Before she could decide what it was she couldn't actually see, he led her into the kitchen. When they reached the dryer he placed her hand on the mound of clothing he'd moved to the top of the machine. Thankful the door didn't have to be opened, thus risking the light giving them away, she fumbled until she found her panties.

Her heart thundering in her chest, she shimmied into the bikinis as the blanket slithered to the floor.

Ethan groaned, but caught himself mid-sound.

She tried to look at him through the blackness, but still couldn't make out any details. "What?" she whispered softly.

"Shhh," he hissed.

She snatched up her bra and glowered at him, for all the good it would do. When she fumbled with the twisted garment he snagged her by the arm and pressed his mouth to her ear again. "We're in a hurry here," he growled.

Abandoning the bra, she grabbed her black T-shirt and cargo pants. She tugged them on in record time. Skipping the socks, she stepped into her still soggy sneakers. Then grabbed the coat and cap.

"I'm ready."

"I can see that," he muttered, his voice strained. "Just one more thing."

He could see? Before she could thoroughly analyze that statement, he smeared something greasy-feeling on her cheeks, her nose and forehead. Without explanation he dragged her toward the back door.

Belatedly, she wondered what time it was.

She rolled her eyes.

Time to run. Time to hide.

On the back stoop the moon provided just enough illumination to define objects. Like Ethan's hulking frame. She wanted to ask him what his plan was, but something else caught her attention. She squinted trying to determine what he wore on his face. The same greasy stuff, she supposed, that he'd smeared on hers. But there was more. He wore something over his eyes. Some sort of strange-looking goggles. The goggles were the shape that she'd made out and thought to be the bill of a cap.

Before she could ask any questions, he bent down and whispered to her once more. "Stay right behind me. Keep your head down. Do not speak. And, for God's sake, don't make any noise."

She considered kicking him to see if he'd make any noise, but since men who wanted to kill them were lurking nearby, she thought better of it. She wanted to live more than she wanted to hurt him.

Ethan moved like a huge, black panther. Sleek, fluid and soundless. She, in contrast, tramped through the ankle-deep grass like an elephant charging through the jungle. Each step she took was accompanied by a soft squishing sound from her wet sneakers.

Ethan stopped.

So did she, her body bumped into his broad back.

He turned to her, laid a finger against his mouth, then froze. Her heart pumped so hard she was certain a coronary episode must be imminent. Did he know how to perform CPR? Would he stop long enough to do it? Most likely his self-preservation instincts outweighed whatever salary the Colby Agency paid him. Besides, if she were dead, he probably wouldn't get paid anyway.

Clearly, she'd lost it. Her weary, confused brain was rambling on overload. She prayed no one could hear the harsh banging in her chest or her ragged, shallow puffs of breath.

Then she heard what Ethan had stopped to listen for.

Voices.

Footsteps.

Close.

Very close.

A scream burgeoned in her throat, making it impossible to breathe or even to think.

The urge to run was so strong, she could scarcely resist the beckoning temptation.

One big hand engulfed hers as if he'd known she wanted to run…to scream. Anything but stand here and wait for the killers to come closer. To…

His fingers wrapped securely around hers and suddenly she remembered the way he'd held her as she drifted off to sleep. The strength in those capable arms, the feel of his powerful body as he'd propelled them both through the rushing water, saving her life... keeping her...safe.

And suddenly she wasn't afraid anymore.

Ethan would protect her.

She'd never known a man like him. Rough and rugged, yet somehow gentle and compassionate.

The voices were louder now.

The two men were going into the house she and Ethan had vacated only minutes ago.

Ethan was moving again. Drawing her forward, keeping her close, her hand still clutched in his.

He led her to a vehicle. She stalled. It was the silver SUV belonging to the men who'd chased them. The men looking for them at this very moment.

"What are we doing?" she demanded, careful to keep her voice low.

He reached through the open driver's-side window and slammed a fist against the center dome light, smashing it, then he opened the door. No tell-tale light shone from the vehicle's interior.

"Get in."

The order was a savage growl.

She scrambled across the driver's seat and console. He was already inside before she could fasten her seat belt. She didn't have the nerve to ask what he was doing. Wasn't even sure she could speak at the moment anyway. If the men came out of the house and saw them...it would be bad.

Very bad.

He did something violent to the steering column.

Though she couldn't see, she could hear. Plastic cracked. Metal slid against metal. Then the engine hummed to life.

Without turning on the headlights, he shifted into gear and rolled slowly down the dark, empty street. The whole world looked asleep around them. They were all alone except for the madmen hoping to track them down like animals.

Ethan removed the strange goggles and shrugged off the backpack as he picked up speed. Both items were tossed onto the floorboard in front of her. They rounded a deep curve, leaving the cottage behind, and he gunned the accelerator. He said nothing.

Adrenaline stung through her, making her pulse react and her already racing heart shudder. "Are you going to turn on the lights now?" she asked, her voice miserably unsteady. She clutched the door...the seat. She was reasonably sure that she wasn't up for another ride like the one they had taken after leaving BalPhar.

"Not yet."

Jenn twisted around in the seat, another wave of panic washing over her. "They're not following us, are they?"

"Nope. And since there weren't any vehicles at any of those cottages, I doubt they'll be able to unless they enjoy a challenging footrace."

She smiled. He'd done it. Yanked them from the jaws of death, yet again. Saved her life.

"My word, but you're good," she enthused. The promise of survival blossomed in her chest.

"We're not home free yet," he warned.

Ever the pessimist, she mused. Her heart rate and blood pressure dropping below stroke level, she leaned back in her seat and tried not to think about the fact that they were flying down a narrow, quiet street, dark houses whizzing by on either side and without any headlights to blaze the way.

The backpack resting at her feet snagged her attention. "The BalPhar files?" A new anxiety speared through her. What if the pages containing her official prints and DNA sequence had been damaged in the river? What would she do then? David would never be stupid enough to allow the same oversight twice. He would destroy any file even remotely related to her.

"I checked everything. No damage except for the cell phone. The plastic evidence bags protected the documents. Bagging evidence is a little habit of mine. Good thing, huh?"

She exhaled the tension that had tightened in her throat. "Oh, yes."

He finally turned on the headlights, peeling away another layer of muscle-knotting tension. The idea that he'd concluded they were home free since he made that concession provided yet another wave of relief.

"See if you can find a cell phone in here somewhere. Maybe one of those guys left theirs. We need new transportation. We have to ditch this SUV."

He was right. By now the two men had probably discovered their mistake and were considering how to rectify it. Using one of the interior sidelights, she quickly scanned the vehicle and located a portable phone. She also noted the time on the digital clock.

Three o'clock. No wonder she was so exhausted, she'd had next to no sleep. She wondered vaguely how Ethan was managing to hold up so well. She doubted he'd gotten any sleep at all.

Ethan told her the number to punch in, then took the phone from her. Turning off the interior light, her gaze caught on the goggles. She picked up the odd eyewear and examined them in the dim glow provided by the illuminated dash as Ethan explained their current situation to someone named Simon. The other guy from the Colby Agency, she remembered. The one he'd planned to have play baby-sitter for her.

"What are these?" she asked when he'd ended the call.

He stared straight ahead for a time before he answered. She watched a little tic begin in his beard-shadowed jaw.

"Night vision."

She frowned at the sound of his taut voice. *Night vision.* The ease with which he moved through the darkness...that groan when she'd dragged on her panties...*I can see that.*

He'd been watching her.

With these goggles.

Anger kindled. "You lowdown—"

"Before you freak out," he cut in smoothly. "Be aware that all objects are somewhat out of focus and green in color when seen through those goggles. I didn't *really* see anything."

She drew back and hit him as hard as she could on

the shoulder with her fist. "Ouch!" she cried, cradling her aching hand.

"I had to get us out of there in a hurry," he argued with a grimace. "There wasn't time to grope around in the dark."

"You could have turned your back while I dressed," she snapped, still massaging her throbbing hand. He hadn't, she was certain about that.

A tiny smile played about the corner of his mouth. The urge to hit him again was palpable.

"You're a dirty old man, Ethan Delaney. What's next? You planning to cop a feel?"

"I did what I had to do," he said flatly.

"And had yourself a little fun at my expense," she argued. "I was scared to death! And all the while you were gawking at my naked body."

He sighed. "What do you want? An apology? Well, forget it. I'm not in the habit of apologizing for saving people's lives."

She muttered the meanest expletive she knew that she felt applied perfectly to him. He just grinned. Oh yes, she definitely wanted to hit him. This was ridiculous. Not once in her entire life had she wanted to do bodily harm to another human being until she met him.

But she did now.

The memory of his mouth covering hers, the feel of his lips suddenly bloomed inside her. He'd kissed her...really kissed her. She was pretty sure he'd at first plastered his mouth over hers to keep her from screaming or speaking. But the gesture had evolved into something else altogether. He'd kissed her for real and she'd kissed him back. Like the time Bogart kissed Ingrid Bergman in that movie, *Casablanca.*

The cellular phone Ethan had abandoned on the console erupted into a symphony of musical notes.

Ethan slowed, his gaze dropping momentarily to the console…to the phone, as did Jenn's.

Then their gazes locked.

"Don't answer it," he ordered.

"What if it's your friend calling back?" Her heart was pounding again.

"It won't be." His tone was so final, so clearly a warning that she shivered.

She snatched up the phone and flipped it open. She had to know who it was. It could be important. A chill went through her as she noted that the identity of the caller had been blocked. But it could be about her father. "Hello."

A lengthy pause.

"*Jennifer.* What a pleasant surprise. Have you and your friend given my men the slip once again?"

The haunting sound of the voice on the other end of the line sent raw fear surging through her veins.

*David.*

Her fingers turned to ice as she clutched the phone to her ear. She shouldn't have answered. She should have listened to Ethan. But something deep inside her wouldn't allow her to hang up. She needed to hear what he had to say. This monster held her father's life in his hands.

"Yes. It's me, darling," he murmured.

Had she said his name out loud? Oh, God. She shuddered. The images from the chapel reeled past her eyes like a bad movie.

"You're making things very difficult. I'm not sure you fully comprehend the consequences of your actions."

Savage, animalian fury suddenly ignited and burned away the fear. "You killed Russ and Dr. Kessler. You...you stole my life! You're a murderer...a thief," her voice faltered with emotion.

Ethan was watching her too closely now, splitting his attention between her and the long inky highway before them. "Jenn," he said, his teeth clenched. "Let me have the phone."

She looked at him. She wanted to do as he said, but she couldn't let go...couldn't *not* listen to what David had to say. It was like passing a horrible accident on the highway, everyone always slowed down and had to look.

"Come home to me now," David demanded, his voice still soft, but his tone menacing.

"I won't let you do this," she warned, the sudden, overwhelming need for vengeance exploding in her chest. "I'm going to get you, David. You'd better find yourself a place to hide because I'm coming." Another first, Jenn realized almost as if standing outside her body and watching herself. She wanted to kill the man she'd just months ago agreed to married. Wanted him dead.

"Careful, darling," David suggested. "I still have the upper hand, you know."

*Her father.*

Please, she prayed, don't let him do this.

"Hang up," Ethan commanded. "Don't listen to anything Crane says."

"I can make his final days on this earth more painful than anything you can imagine," David whispered. "Excruciating. As he takes his final breath, he will know that he has you to thank for it."

A horrifying moment of desperate silence followed.

She couldn't speak, couldn't plead with him to spare her father. Her heart was lodged firmly in her throat, still pounding, cutting off her breath, making speech impossible. How could she stop him?

She couldn't. No one could.

Her frantic gaze swung in Ethan's direction.

Not even Ethan could stop this. They had no legal recourse at this point…there was nothing they could do. She couldn't prove any of his wrong doing. Uncle Russ's body had obviously been done away with.

"You have twenty-four hours to come home to me, or your father will pay the price." David paused, then added, "If Delaney interferes, I will kill him. Don't doubt my word."

He disconnected.

She stared at the phone in her hand.

Ethan snatched it from her and threw it into the back of the vehicle.

"What did the bastard say?"

Ethan's voice was a full-fledged roar now.

"Nothing," she whispered. Defeat sagged her shoulders. It was over. "Nothing important."

Ethan looked from the road to her and back. ''You're sure about that?''

She nodded.

She couldn't tell Ethan the truth. He would never allow her to follow David's orders.

And that was the only choice she had.

She couldn't let him hurt her father.

*Chapter Ten*

As the pink and purple hues of the rising sun reached above the treetops a few hours later, Jenn stood in the dimly lit living room before the wall of east-facing windows in Max's cabin. She'd survived another day, by the grace of God and Ethan Delaney. She owed him so very much. Above all, he'd believed her and kept her from going through the last couple of days alone. But all his efforts would be for nothing.

Simon Ruhl, a dark, mysterious man with short-cropped black hair and eyes so dark they were almost black, had met them just inside the Chicago city limits with new transportation. They'd left the silver SUV in an area on the south side known for stripping and stealing cars. Within an hour of leaving the vehicle, it had likely been dismantled beyond recognition. That would buy them some time, Ethan had said. Throw the hunters off their trail since the vehicle would be less easily identified when it was discovered.

He'd also said that Simon would be watching their backs for a while, whatever that meant. The moment they returned to the cabin, Ethan had faxed the BalPhar files to Lucas Camp. Lucas assured Ethan that no one at his lab would rest until the job was done.

There was no time to waste. Unless the results from the DNA and fingerprint analysis came in before midnight tonight and offered irrefutable evidence that she was Jennifer Ballard, her life was over. To that end, she'd made some advance preparations.

She would not risk a moment longer than that. David might change his mind about giving her the full twenty-four hours. If the results were not available by midnight, she would go to him. She closed her eyes and banished the images that thought conjured, but the emotions that accompanied that inevitable fate weren't so easily conquered. Feeling this level of hatred rattled her, disgusted her.

She forced her eyes open and drew in a deep, bolstering breath. There were two things she had to do before she surrendered. One, she had to devise a plan to escape from Ethan since she was certain he would never allow her to go near David Crane. Second, she had to be with Ethan. *Really be with him.*

If this was her last day on earth, she intended to make the most of it. Making love with Ethan was the one thing she could not bear leaving this world without having experienced. She wanted to touch him, taste him and have him do the same to her in every imaginable way, and maybe even some she hadn't thought of. She might not be experienced sexually, but she knew what she wanted. All it took was one look at him and she burned for his touch. She imagined he had that effect on most women.

The fact that she would never be able to follow in her father's pioneering footsteps didn't really matter anymore. Her priorities had changed drastically in the past week. Faced with certain death, nothing really felt that important now other than assuring that her father was not made to suffer, and being with Ethan. She couldn't be sure whether she could trust David to be as good as his word where her father was concerned, but that was a risk she would have to take. She loved her father too much to take any chances. She cared too much about Ethan as well. No way would she allow David to hurt him. She had to protect Ethan at all costs, just as she had to protect her father.

Ethan mattered a great deal to her. More than she could ever have imagined. She wanted desperately to be with him. The depth of the need was more intense than any other emotion she'd ever experienced. Though she couldn't quite label the way he made her feel, she wanted to be with him…to be close that way. The fondness she felt for him was fierce. Breath-stealing.

She wanted to understand it, to explore it. Though time was short and she might not come to a full understanding, she had every intention of giving it her best shot. All she had to do was convince him.

With her mind made up, she climbed the stairs to the second floor. He'd allowed her to shower first. Washing away the scent of that murky river had felt marvelous. Then Ethan had taken his turn, skirting wide around her outside the bathroom door. He'd seen her in a towel before, she didn't understand what the big deal was. Well, she paused midway up the stairs, that wasn't completely true, she admitted. *The rules.* Getting involved on a personal level with a client was against the rules. Under normal circumstances, it was the sensible thing, she supposed. But her circumstances were far from normal. Her number was up. She was a goner. What did the rules matter now?

As she resumed her climb up the staircase the sound of spraying water in the shower abruptly halted. She cursed herself for not making up her mind sooner. She would have liked to join him in the shower. Too late for that now. Okay, she'd improvise.

He'd left the bathroom door open, she noted when she took the last step up. To keep an ear out for her, no doubt. Ever the protector. He had every intention of keeping her safe. Then all thought ceased for one explosive second when he stepped from the shower.

He was gloriously naked. Her breath trapped in her lungs as she moved silently across the expanse of carpeted floor. He was vigorously drying his long hair with the towel. This was the first time she'd ever seen it loose.

Her gaze traveled down that amazing torso, sculpted and sleek with just the barest hint of silken hair scattered over his chest. His hips were lean and narrow and flowed into muscular thighs. Her gaze jerked back to his semi-aroused loins. Her mouth parched. The man was seriously endowed. Not quite a scientific phenomenon, but close. Very close.

She moistened her lips, clamping down on her lower one to prevent the little sound of approval that threatened to leap from her mouth. She should have expected that, she supposed, judging by his massive physical build. He was definitely a prime example of the species.

Halfway across the room she stalled again as he lowered the towel and turned to see who was there as if he'd heard her, which was impossible because, for once, she hadn't made a sound. Maybe he'd sensed her presence. Though clothed in the borrowed nightshirt, she felt suddenly naked beneath that slow, intense stare.

His hair was tousled, but looked completely awesome loose, falling just past his shoulders. She shivered as a spear of heat arced through her. That handsome face was free of the stubble that had darkened it. The lines and angles of that chiseled terrain made her pulse trip. He was so good-looking. So strong. And no tattoo. She smiled.

"Did you need something?" he asked, a new kind of tension in his voice. He lowered the towel in his hands until it camouflaged his spectacular manhood.

Those dark eyes watched every subtle shift of her body, her expression. He knew what she wanted. He wanted it as well. She could see it in his eyes...in the response of his splendidly defined masculine body. But he wanted to resist. She could see that as well. His posture was rigid, guarded. Wariness had slipped into his eyes.

"Yes," she said in answer to his question. She did need something.

The towel still strategically located, he started toward her. Met her just outside the bathroom door...two or three feet from the inviting bed with its well-polished wooden posts, its soft, wide mattress.

His hooded gaze settled heavily onto hers. "I never get personally involved with a client," he told her, his voice soft and at the same time, rough with a sensuality that came as naturally as breathing. "It's against the rules."

*Damn the rules.*

"I don't want you to get personally involved with me," she said, her voice oddly calm and strong considering the whirlwind of emotions twisting within her. Her body was hot and throbbing. She felt ready to combust. She was also just a little afraid of what would come next. But she was even more terrified that it might not. "I want you to make love to me, that's all."

He tunneled the fingers of one hand through his silky hair, taming it somewhat. "You're young and confused with all that's going on in your life right now. You're not thinking clearly. It's not me you want." His fingers fisted in the towel once more. "It's a distraction you need."

"What's wrong with a distraction between consenting adults?" she asked, surprised at how steady her voice sounded when she was quaking inside.

He shook his head slowly, then gestured vaguely to her. "The first time should be savored, saved for a special moment. You'll only regret it later."

He couldn't know that for her there would be no later.

"Let me get dressed and we'll think of something to do." He shrugged one of those broad shoulders, the flex of smooth skin and powerful muscle adding to her mounting tension. "We can talk, or something."

"I don't want to talk." She looked directly at him, hoping to convey the depth of her determination.

He held up a hand to halt her when she would have moved toward him a step. "I don't want you to regret anything between us," he said softly. "This moment should be shared with the man you intend to spend the rest of your life with."

*That would be you,* she didn't say.

Moving closer to him, first one step, then another, she dragged the nightshirt up and off, then dropped it to the floor. "This *is* a special moment, and I don't want to let it pass."

The heart that had been hammering in Ethan's chest skidded to a complete halt. In that endless nanosecond before it kicked back into gear, he surveyed the nearly naked woman before him. He told himself to look away, but that wasn't happening this side of the grave. The night vision definitely had not done her justice. Her skin was smooth and creamy, pale in comparison to his. She was so slender...so fragile looking. Her breasts were perfect. Small, but firm and so damned perky he could hardly restrain the temptation to reach out and touch one.

He swallowed hard as his gaze slid down her flat abdomen. Tiny bikini panties were all that stood between him and seeing every square inch of her. And he wanted to see all of her...wanted to have her. He gritted his teeth and forced the thought away.

"Jenn—"

Whatever he'd intended to say vacated his brain the instant she pushed the bikini panties down her thighs, taking her time, and allowing them to drag against her flesh. She shivered visibly. He clenched his fists. A familiar ache started to build inside him. She tossed the skimpy panties aside and advanced on him once more.

"Don't make this harder than it needs to be," he warned, pleaded actually. From his perspective things were already damned hard.

She reached out, cool fingers splayed over his chest. "At least let me touch you."

Like he could stop her. He could barely hold back from grabbing her and throwing her across the bed now. Right this second. "That's not a good idea." He drew her hand away from his chest, difficult as that was.

Her intent expression crumpled. Her eyes widened. "You don't want me?" The surprise and hurt in her voice told him she'd only just considered that idea.

He quickly slung the towel around his waist so both hands would be free. "No," he assured her softly. "It's not that. I told you—"

"To hell with the rules," she argued, anger blazing in her eyes now. "I know what I want. I'm an adult. Don't treat me like a child."

Ethan swore. Though he firmly considered her too young and naive for a guy like him, he knew with complete certainty that she was a woman. If she only knew just how much he wanted her. He sighed and closed his eyes for one beat. He didn't just want her in the physical sense. Her safety, her well-being was important to him.

Hell, it was even more than that. *She* was important to him. He refused to analyze that bit of irony. This wasn't supposed to happen. He hadn't felt this kind of need in a very long time. Not since the only woman he'd ever loved left him.

"Ethan."

He opened his eyes. Jenn stared up at him with such tender desire in her eyes that his soul ached to take her in his arms. But he couldn't.

"I won't take no for an answer. I want this." She tiptoed and brushed her lips across his, the gesture so damned sweet and innocent he wanted to roar with the want gripping him.

"We don't have any protection," he countered, grasping at straws, his voice uneven and breathless. He couldn't hold out much longer. If he didn't change her mind soon, it would be over. He'd lose...or win, depending on how one looked at it. What the hell was he thinking? He couldn't do this.

"Do you usually practice safe sex?" she inquired, her fingers trailing down his torso in a most distracting manner.

His loins throbbed. He tried his level best to maintain control, but it was growing more difficult by the second. She was so beautiful. Her slender body was exquisite. Soft, feminine, and untouched. He swallowed convulsively again. He wanted to take her. To claim her as his own.

"I always practice safe sex," he muttered in answer to her question. He was suddenly unsure as to whether he was sweating or simply still damp from the shower. Just looking at her, having her touch him in such an innocent fashion was driving him so crazy that his money was on sweat.

"Then we don't have a problem," she announced, coming boldly closer. "I'm a virgin. I've practiced the safest sex of all."

Okay, that was it. He was on the verge of throwing her across the bed and giving her exactly what she asked for. She'd had him as hard as a rock from the moment she took off her clothes in that cottage after their little river adventure. Spending almost an hour in his arms on that scruffy old couch hadn't helped. The little shimmy into her panties while he watched with the night vision had all but finished him off. But that had been his own fault. He should have looked away. But he couldn't.

"But there could be other complications," he argued, grabbing back sanity. Relief, so profound he all but staggered, surged through him. He had her there. He doubted she was on the pill since she was unmarried and not sexually active.

She shook head, her long golden tresses shifting around her delicate shoulders. If only he could touch all that silky stuff.

"At this stage in my cycle, pregnancy is not likely."

God have mercy on him. She'd thought of everything.

"Jenn, you—"

She tugged the towel from his hips and tossed it aside. She looked at him, then she touched him again. Touched him intimately.

He groaned. "Jenn." He tried without success to pull her hands away. "I know you're not thinking this through. One of us has to be rational. I don't want you to get hurt.'' He gritted his teeth against another groan as those soft fingers encircled him.

She pressed her body against his, her softness only making him harder when he'd thought it was impossible. The feel of her breasts against his bare chest made his entire body jerk with need.

''If you don't want to hurt me, then shut up and show me what I've been missing.''

He would have at least attempted to argue further, but she tiptoed again and shushed him with her mouth. She kissed him so innocently he could scarcely bear the sweetness of it. Still, he held back. Her hands slid up his chest and around his neck. She arched her hips against him.

''Now,'' she murmured. ''I don't want to wait any longer.''

When he hesitated, she urged, ''Show me how to make love.''

In one swift-as-lightning move, he swept her into his arms and deposited her on the bed. He lowered his body next to hers and fell into the kiss he'd denied himself moments before.

He teased her lips for what felt like forever, then pried them open and delved inside. She whimpered and arched against him. His hand slipped down to her breast, another move she approved of. The firm globe filled his palm, made him yearn to taste her. And he did. He took one pebbled nipple into his mouth and sucked long and hard. She cried out. He did the same with the other breast, eliciting more sounds of desire from her.

Those slender hips undulated against him, driving him absolutely mad. He had to slow her down, draw out the pleasure. His hand glided down her ribcage, tracing, learning the delicate curves and hollows. He touched her downy-soft hair, trailed one finger along her quivering feminine channel.

She arched against his hand, spread her thighs in anticipation of his touch. He continued to torture her breasts with his mouth as he teased those sweet feminine lips. His own need flamed higher, building like an inferno. He dipped a finger inside her, testing, teasing. She stilled. Another finger slipped in. He stretched her, gently plying her tight sheath, preparing her for what was to come.

He knew he should stop this before things went any further, but he simply did not have the willpower to refuse her. She'd pushed him beyond the point of reason. He rubbed her swollen bud of desire with the heel of his hand. She moaned loudly and thrashed wildly beneath his onslaught. She was so hot. So tight. It took all his powers of concentration not to erupt against her soft, warm flesh.

She reached for him, encircled his swollen shaft as she'd done before. Her fingers were soft and cool. She massaged up and down. He groaned savagely, helplessly. He wanted to be inside her. Now. But it was too soon. He wanted her wetter, hotter.

He made a path down her belly with his tongue. Lapping, twirling, nibbling with his teeth. When he reached her mound, she opened further for him as if she'd known what he intended…as if she couldn't wait to discover more. He tasted her, his fingers kneading her thighs, her buttocks. She cried out his name, surged upward against his mouth. He teased and licked and suckled until she screamed with delight, her inner muscles pulsing around his tongue.

*Now* she was ready.

She was begging him to take her, not with words, but with her sweet body.

"Ethan, please," she murmured, giving voice to what her body was already saying. If Jenn lived another moment without him inside her, it would be a miracle. He was driving her insane. Her heart pounded, tried to burst from her chest. She couldn't catch her breath. Her body felt hot and achy all over. Wave after wave of intense pleasure was washing over her. She'd never felt such powerful sensations before.

He kneed her legs apart, lowered his body between them, nudged her entrance. She moaned from the sweet agony of it. He teased her, rubbing against her, but didn't thrust. She wrapped her legs around his and arched, wanting, needing. He rubbed his length along her femininity, denying her what she yearned for.

"Please," she murmured again, desperate.

Then came the exquisite sensation of penetration. Slowly…so very slowly that her heart seemed to stop completely, he entered her, one slow, hot inch at a time. It was the most spectacular feeling she'd ever experienced. She opened her eyes and stared up at him, wanting to see, to add another layer of awareness to this perfect moment.

Suddenly he stopped, held stone-still. Frantic for

more of him, she whimpered her disapproval. Those dark eyes opened and peered down at her. The intensity on his handsome face sent butterflies soaring throughout her. The same desire she felt, every bit as fierce, was mirrored in his eyes. He was breathing hard and fast. His muscles taut with restraint. A thin line of perspiration stretched across his forehead. She could feel him throbbing, pressing against the thin tissue of her virginity.

"You're sure about this?" His voice was rough, guttural. The sound skittered across her nerve endings, making her quiver uncontrollably.

She looked deeply into those questioning eyes and smiled. Reaching up to touch his face, she whispered, "Yes."

Ethan could wait no longer.

He'd tried to do the honorable thing.

Helpless now, he could only do what he yearned to with his entire being.

He almost climaxed when he forced past the barrier that confirmed her as untouched. She cried out…or he did…or both. A sense of possessiveness claimed him, made him suddenly dizzy.

She was his.

The emotion startled him a little at first. The feeling of raw, primal possessiveness was so keen it was almost painful. No other man could ever touch her now.

*She was his.*

Her hips surged upward, completing the seal between their bodies and taking him completely. He held still for two long beats, savoring the feel of her around him like a second skin, and giving her tight body time to adjust to his size.

When enough time had passed, he rocked gently. Moving slowly. In. Out. He groaned hoarsely at the feel of her hot, slick flesh dragging along his length. He was so close to the edge, but he wanted to take her with him.

"Ethan," she murmured, her cool fingers clenching and unclenching on his back.

Her eyes were closed in ecstasy. He drew back, all the way to the tip, far enough to taste one breast in his mouth. He sucked hard. She squirmed, moaning, arching her back and urging him on with her frantic hands.

She was building toward climax, whimpering, writhing, pleading with him to do something she couldn't name. He nuzzled forward a fraction, withdrew, nudged forward. She gripped his shoulders and pulled him closer. Still, he held back. When he felt her tremors begin, he surged forth in one long stroke. She stiffened beneath him and he repeated the movement. She screamed. Again and again, he thrust fully, deeply, until she convulsed around him. Every tiny ripple squeezed his hardened flesh, propelled him toward release. The feeling was so intense he could hardly breathe, couldn't think at all. He could only act on his most primal, basic instincts. To mate with her, to claim her as his own, to take her to that pinnacle once more as he climbed higher and higher, his physical enjoyment mounting as never before.

Stars suddenly burst behind his tightly clenched lids. Release erupted from him so savagely he cried out. His fingers fisted in the sheets, his face contorted with the pleasure-pain.

He slowed, drawing out the last remnants of her release. He peered down at her angelic face, her sweet mouth. The words he had not spoken in over a decade rushed to the tip of his tongue, but he held them back. This wasn't supposed to happen. Not like this. He shouldn't feel any of this.

But he did.

She gasped, then sighed and went limp, further disrupting his ability to think. Her fingers feathered along his back, his sides, leaving a trail of fire.

She smiled up at him. "Can we do that again?"

He forced those crazy emotions aside and focused on giving the woman in his arms complete satisfaction. He wasn't any good with all that emotional crap anyway. But he was very, very good at this.

He went deep. She gasped. He took her hands in his, held them above her head, dominating, repressing those softer feelings. He kissed her mouth, then murmured, "We can definitely do it again."

HER PLAN WOULD WORK. She knew it would. She'd hidden a change of clothes downstairs in the kitchen before...

The vivid details of making love with Ethan tumbled into her head, taking her breath, stealing her courage. How could she have known that it would be that beautiful...that amazing? Her heart was breaking already at the thought of what she had to do. But there was no way to change it.

She had to go.

She was the only hope her father had.

He would do the same for her.

She descended the stairs slowly, so as not to make Ethan suspicious. She'd asked him to fill the large garden tub so that they could bathe together while she went downstairs for something cold to drink. She would return with two longneck bottles of beer in minutes, she'd assured him.

All she had to do was jump into her clothes and get out the back door before he realized she'd been gone longer than necessary. She'd memorized the security code. She'd be in the new SUV and out of here before he realized what she'd done and gotten his own clothes on.

She grabbed the keys from the table at the bottom of the staircase and ran for the kitchen. In less than one minute, she had on her jeans, T-shirt and shoes. The abandoned nightshirt lay on the floor.

Holding her breath for fear he'd suddenly appear behind her, she entered the security code. The pad beeped and flashed the Disarmed warning. Slowly, holding her breath again, she turned the knob. The door opened. She slipped out and closed it softly behind her.

It took Jenn a full five seconds to gather her composure as she battled the consequences of her actions one last time. She was going to die. But she had no choice. She'd actually planned to wait until midnight tonight, but after this morning's lovemaking she'd realized two things: Every moment she spent with Ethan would make it harder for her to leave him. She might break down and tell him everything. She couldn't risk that. Second, she had to act while he was at his most vulnerable.

And that was now.

She would contact Victoria at various times through-out the day about the DNA and fingerprint analysis. If the results were in her favor she would give Ethan her location and they would take David down together. If the results were not favorable, then she would go to David while Ethan remained safe. She would hide out until then—while she still had the courage to leave. A few more minutes in Ethan's arms and she wouldn't be able to go.

She ran as fast as she could toward the SUV. She skidded to a stop at the driver's side and fumbled with the keys. She'd deactivated the lock and had reached for the door when a deep male voice stopped her.

"Good morning, Jennifer."

## Chapter Eleven

"Have you totally lost your mind?"

Even though she'd fully expected him to yell at her, Jenn jumped when Ethan asked the question.

"I'll just get back to my post now," Simon Ruhl said in that deep, baritone voice of his from near the door.

Jenn didn't blame him. She'd forgo this next few minutes herself if possible. At least now she knew what Ethan had meant when he said that Simon would be watching their backs. He'd been outside, his vehicle camouflaged in the trees, watching the cabin. She'd never had a chance of getting away.

"Thanks, Simon." Ethan exhaled, clearly grappling for a calm that was currently elusive.

The half smile Simon sent in Ethan's and then in her direction before disappearing out the door, told her that Simon knew exactly what was going on here.

Ethan's hair was still tousled. He was shirtless and his jeans had been hastily pulled on. Even under present circumstances, her throat went dry as she considered that magnificent chest and those snug-fitting jeans. The scent of their lovemaking still clung to his skin, as well as her own. In spite of everything, already she ached for him again.

But she couldn't think about that now. She had to focus on the next step—helping her father and, somehow, in the process keeping Ethan clear of the danger. Tears burned the backs of her eyes as David's threat echoed in her ears. She'd been selfish for a few hours this morning, now it was time to do what she knew she had to.

It was the only way to help her father...to keep Ethan from falling victim to the same fate as Russ and Kessler.

"I should have taken you to Melbourne," he snapped. "You're obviously out of your mind."

Melbourne? She frowned. *The shrink.* "I'm not crazy."

He looked unconvinced. Furious.

She could see his point at the moment, she supposed. But she still didn't understand why he'd brought up Melbourne before. Maybe... Enlightenment dawned. The little breakdown—that really wasn't a breakdown at all—that she'd suffered when she was fifteen. She narrowed her gaze. "Haven't you ever just lost it? Then needed time to pull yourself back together so you could get on with it?"

The grim set to his mouth before he looked away answered her question. "We're not talking about me."

What demons haunted his past? she wondered. She closed her eyes for a moment. But that really wasn't the problem right now, was it?

When Ethan's formidable gaze settled on hers once more, she moistened her lips, expelled a heavy breath and told him the truth. "If I don't go back to David, he's going to make my father suffer.'' It amazed her that her voice didn't sound nearly as shaky as she felt. She'd rushed out of the house this morning, her courage shored up by Ethan's tender lovemaking. But now she felt like a spent party balloon, useless and unnecessary.

Renewed fury flashed in those dark eyes. ''You were going back to Crane?''

His voice was a beast-like roar. She tried to analyze the mixture of emotions behind it, but couldn't quite sort them all out. She was nearly certain something that sounded distinctly like possessiveness, or jealousy maybe, was there.

Perched on the edge of the sofa, she braced herself for another blast of his fury. ''There's no other way. He gave me twenty-four hours. If I can't get the proof I need to bring him down or turn myself in to him, he'll torture my father.'' She swiped fiercely at the single tear that escaped her tight hold on composure. She would not cry. She had to be strong. ''And if you get in the way, he said he'd kill you.''

Ethan swore. A number of words she had not heard before. All of which made her blush.

''You had twenty-four hours. Why didn't you tell me about this so we could take some sort of action?'' he demanded as he stormed in her direction. He towered over her now, for effect, she felt confident.

He arched an eyebrow. ''And I'm a big boy, I can take care of myself. I don't need some little—'' He caught himself, just barely. Something in his eyes changed, softened for just the briefest moment. ''I don't need you to fight my battles.''

Did he not realize that there was no decision to be

made? Her mind was made up. She spoke slowly. It was immensely important that he understood just how dire the situation was. "Russ is dead. Kessler is dead. I have no proof that Cellneu is dangerous so I can't approach the situation from that avenue. And, as if that isn't bad enough, I can't prove who I am, so I can't simply walk in and order him off the premises of my own home…my own company. I don't have a choice." She prayed he would understand. "Sure I could stir up trouble, but that wouldn't protect my father. The only way my father is going to be safe from David is if I return."

She wondered now if she took one of those big guns Ethan carried, perhaps she could square things with David herself. She shuddered inwardly. Yes, she wanted revenge, that was true enough. She wanted it in the worst way. She wanted it Old Testament-style.

Ethan shook his head, his glare only intensifying. "You didn't trust me enough to tell me." He sat down on the coffee table, braced his arms on his knees, putting himself at her eye level. "I won't let anything happen to you or your father. All you have to do is trust me." He looked away for a moment. "Even after what we shared this morning, you couldn't trust me enough to tell me?"

She did trust him, and she desperately wanted to believe he could protect her father. But, as strong and capable as Ethan was, David had too many men ready to obey his orders. One man couldn't stop them all.

"Don't you see," she urged. "He's waiting for me. He'll be watching. If you try to come near the house or the company, he'll have you killed. He'll hurt my invalid father. I can't take that risk. I have to do this alone.''

He looked ready to belt out another stream of those violent curses, but he refrained, the tremendous effort it took visible. ''Before the twenty-four hours are up,'' he said in a reasonably calm tone, ''we might have the DNA or fingerprint evidence we need to put you back in control. Why didn't you at least wait for those results?''

This was the tricky part. If she said the wrong thing now... ''I knew you'd be watching me too closely later. Especially if the results didn't go my way. I wasn't going to surrender to David until the results were in and it was obvious I had no other alternative. But it was imperative that I left this morning or...or lose my nerve.''

Ethan was too smart for her evasive tactics. The look in his eyes made her want to run for cover. ''So you made your move while I was distracted,'' he suggested, his voice stone-cold.

Even the fury in his eyes couldn't cover the disappointment, the hurt she'd wielded. She hadn't meant to do that. ''Yes.''

A heart-wrenching silence lengthened between them while their gazes remained locked in battle.

Ethan was the first to look away. ''Jenn—''

The ringing of the telephone cut off the rest of his words. He looked at her for the space of one more ring. Then, without another word, he stood and went to answer the phone. She closed her eyes against the image of his muscular back. The same one she'd learned so intimately just a couple of hours ago.

"Delaney."

It dawned on her suddenly that it might be Lucas Camp with the results of the tests.

The tension already tightening her chest torqued a little tighter.

"How can that be?"

That question sent her anxiety level through the roof. What did he mean, *how can that be?*

"Yeah. Fax me a copy. Thanks, Lucas. If you find out anything else, let me know."

When Ethan hung up the phone, she was so paralyzed by fear that she couldn't ask the question that burned in her brain.

He turned to face her. Would have to have been blind not to see the fear in her eyes.

"It was a match."

The words were spoken so quietly that at first she wasn't sure if she'd heard right.

"A match?"

She was afraid to hope.

He nodded.

She couldn't take a deep breath. Couldn't make herself move though she wanted to stand…to move closer to him…have him hold her and tell her that everything would be all right now.

"Both samples," he began, "yours and hers, matched the prints and the DNA sequence from the BalPhar files."

*Both?*

But that was impossible. It had to be a trick. David had somehow done this. She was sure of it.

"That can't be right. He must have tampered with—''

Ethan moved in her direction, sat down on the table across from her again, and took her hands in his. "Her prints, her DNA match yours identically."

Jenn could only shake her head. "It's impossible."

"You're certain this woman isn't related to you? Could there be a sister that you don't know about?" he offered, his fingers softly caressing her hands in a soothing manner.

She shook her head again. "No. There's no one. I'm certain." She pulled her hands free of his. "But simply being my sister wouldn't be enough. If her DNA sequence is the same, exactly the same, and her prints are a perfect match, then she'd have to be my twin." She pressed him with her gaze. "An identical twin. I would know about an identical twin."

"They're looking into other possibilities," Ethan explained. "Lucas's facilities are the most advanced on the planet. If his people don't know of a way to invoke a phenomenon like this, I doubt anyone does. Could Crane have been working on some way to falsify DNA?"

She shrugged. It was the twenty-first century, most anything was possible. "We have all kinds of DNA research going on, but I don't recall anything like this." Her gaze collided with his. "What're we going to do? If I can't prove I'm the real Jennifer Ballard, I can't stop him."

"We'll have to approach this from the Cellneu standpoint then." He sat up straighter. She could almost see the wheels turning in that handsome head. "BalPhar has to have files. Somewhere Crane has some sort of documentation about the hazards. Or, at the very least, falsified documentation that we can prove has been tampered with."

Her head was starting to spin again. David was going to win. Her father would be made to suffer and she would lose her whole world.

"It's true then," she murmured. "I can't stop him." Her heart sank all the way to her sneakers.

He took her hands in his once more. "We have to find out where Crane got this look-alike. She's the key—"

"There's no time. My father is too ill already. If David hurts him, it may kill him and I'll never get to see him again."

"Then we have to stop Crane. We need the BalPhar files." Ethan thought for a moment. "I'll find another way in. I'll get the files."

"But I'm the one who knows where everything is," she argued. It would be the most efficient for her to be the one to go in.

"And you'll tell me exactly where to look," he countered.

She sighed and threaded her fingers through her hair. "There's no time. We have to move now."

"I agree, but we have to make our move the right one."

Exactly what she had to do was suddenly crystal-clear. "As you said before," she said, the idea gaining momentum, "*she's* the key. Without her, he can't get away with it."

Ethan's expression suddenly closed, his guard went

up. "Kidnapping is a felony," he reminded her, his tone all business, the old Ethan now. Not the one who had made love to her so thoroughly.

Jenn felt a smile tugging across her lips. "We don't want to kidnap her. We just want to distract her for a little while." That was it! She had it! All she had to do was take the impostor's place for a few hours and she could get the files. She would impersonate the impostor. Ha! It was a perfect plan.

"It won't work," Ethan said dryly.

"It will work." She shot to her feet, scooted past Ethan to pace the room. "Simon can help us. He can distract her while I go to BalPhar pretending to be her." Jenn glanced at her watch, then remembered the day of the week. "It's perfect. Today is the second Wednesday of the month. David will be meeting with the Sacred Heart Foundation today. He'll be out of the office all afternoon. The timing couldn't be better. Once I have the papers in my hands we can go for my father."

Ethan pushed to his feet and followed her every step with his eyes. "It's too risky. I'll go in. I can devise a cover. I'll only need a little time to prepare."

"We don't have time. We go in now."

He plowed a hand through his hair. "Then I'll go in with you."

She walked up to him, laid her hand against that magnificent chest and pleaded with him with her eyes. "We have to do this my way, Ethan. It's the *only* way."

LESS THAN two hours later, Ethan sat in the SUV, with Jenn next to him. They listened to the conversation Simon was having with the other Jennifer Ballard.

Ethan couldn't help a grin when he considered how charming Simon could be. And Victoria thought Ethan was the one who had a way with the ladies.

They had followed the impostor to a ritzy boutique. Simon had captured the lady's attention by mentioning that he was looking for a present for his girlfriend. The flirtatious ''other'' Jenn was more than glad to assist him. Though the inflection was a little off, the woman's voice was uncanny. Very close to that of the real Jennifer Ballard's.

Jenn sat in the passenger seat, rendered silent by the eerie voice drifting from the receiver's speaker. Simon had bought the lady a drink at the upscale boutique's bar. He had added a little something to the yuppie concoction to take her out of the picture for a few hours. It was harmless. She would wake up in a hotel room, wondering why she'd agreed to accompany a stranger to his room. Simon would watch her until Jenn was out of BalPhar with the files.

And Ethan would be watching her. He would be right behind her and listening in since Jenn also wore a wire.

Ethan didn't like any of this. He didn't like it one bit. But she was right, they had no other choice. Crane had left them no choice.

Before Ethan could worry any further about the idea of Jenn going back into BalPhar, Simon gave them their cue. He'd just accompanied the impostor to the dressing-room area.

''Let's go.''

Jenn smiled, but it was dim and far too shaky for Ethan's comfort. They exited the vehicle and walked past Simon's sedan, moving quietly toward the rear entrance of the boutique. One tap on the door marked Employees Only and it opened.

"There's a persistent saleslady who keeps sticking her head in to see if we need any help," Simon said quickly, "so make it fast."

Ethan nodded. He waited in the empty dressing stall next to the one where the impostor now snoozed. Simon waited in a chair in the mirrored viewing area he'd been shown to by the saleslady. Jenn was already in the stall changing clothes with the impostor.

Two minutes ticked by.

"You okay?" Ethan murmured, his forehead pressed against the thin wall that divided the dressing stalls.

Pause. "Yes."

He could hear the rustle of fabric and the whisper of a sliding zipper.

Ethan swallowed hard. Tension knotted in his stomach. He couldn't lose this woman. He'd suffered that kind of loss once. He wasn't sure his heart could take that much damage again. Maria hadn't been able to deal with his job and he hadn't understood. He'd thought she would come around. But she hadn't. He'd left on that last mission when she'd begged him not to go. When he'd returned, Maria was gone. He'd lost her because he couldn't *not* do his job.

Maybe he could have talked her into coming back…made things right, except she'd gotten killed in a car accident on the way back to her home state of Florida. She'd packed her bags, climbed into that little Volkswagen of hers and hit the road. And she'd died because he'd put his career before her. The next mission he'd taken he'd gone out of his way to get himself killed.

For more than a year, he'd blamed himself and wallowed in self-pity. He'd eventually given up his career and done nothing except bury his head in the sand. Then Victoria had called, made him an offer he couldn't refuse and he hadn't looked back since.

He hadn't allowed himself to get that close to anyone else. Until now.

He couldn't let Jenn get away from him. He'd almost told her that when she'd asked him if he'd never lost it. But now wasn't the time. They had a lot of talking to do, about a lot of things. And now, she was poised to risk everything.

"We should rethink this plan," he said, the sudden urge to grab her and run out of the place nearly overpowering.

"We're fine for the moment," Simon said abruptly, loudly.

Ethan tensed. He heard the low monotone of the saleslady.

"We'll try the black one next," Simon suggested.

Silence.

"It's clear." He tapped on Jenn's dressing-room door. "We're cutting this a little close. You ready yet?"

Ethan heard the dressing-room door open. He quickly emerged from the one he'd hidden in. He blinked as he looked at the woman who'd walked through that back door with him. Wearing the pale-blue suit the impostor had worn into the boutique, Jenn looked exactly like her. She'd even restyled her hair.

"Let's get her out of here," Simon suggested, nodding to the dressing room where the impostor slumped in one corner.

Ethan grabbed Jenn by the arm and pulled her close. "If *anything* feels wrong, I want you out of there. Don't think twice. Just do it. All you have to do is say the word and I'll be there to help you."

He didn't give her time to answer, he kissed her. Kissed her hard and fast. "I'm not letting anything happen to you," he murmured before letting her go.

Simon cleared his throat in warning.

Ethan hefted the lady now wearing Jenn's jeans and T-shirt over his shoulder and hurried out the back door. He dumped the impostor into the back seat of Simon's sedan, then climbed into the SUV and put his earpiece into place. His heart was pounding. God, he didn't want her to do this.

For the first time in his life he understood the helplessness Maria had felt. Jenn could be walking into a death trap. If for some reason Crane came back early from that meeting, he would likely figure out she wasn't the woman he'd wed. The possibility burned in Ethan's chest, made him want to storm back into that boutique and drag her out of there.

But if he did, she would never forgive him. She wanted her father safe from Crane.

Ethan had to help her accomplish that. And more. They had to bring down Crane. Get Jenn her life back…and go from there. Ethan didn't want to think about where they would be then. This was work. He shouldn't have gotten involved with a client. It was a mistake. Against the rules. He knew better.

"No thanks, this one will be fine," Jenn said, her voice clear and steady in Ethan's ear.

The saleslady had obviously returned.

"Would you like to look at anything else, baby?" Simon asked for the saleslady's benefit.

His tone, the idea that he might have his arm around Jenn or his hand at the small of her back sent a stab of jealousy deep into Ethan's gut. He shook his head. Damn, he had it bad here.

Simon paid for the dress. The saleslady asked them to come again. Ethan heard the jingle of the bell as Simon and Jenn left the store through the front doors. Ethan eased closer to the street. He could see Jenn now, standing near the waiting car. She and Simon exchanged good-byes and he started in Ethan's direction.

Jenn hesitated before getting into the car. For one long moment, she simply stood there staring toward Ethan. She was afraid.

"Watch my back." The words were a mere murmur in his earpiece.

"I'll be right behind you." Ethan drew in a ragged breath as she climbed into the back seat of the waiting car. So many things could go wrong. The darkly tinted windows prevented him from seeing inside. But he knew the impostor had arrived alone. That was the one good thing in all this.

Simon walked right past the SUV without looking Ethan's way so as not to draw attention to his position. In his driver's-side mirror, Ethan saw Simon slide behind the wheel of the sedan. He would head to the hotel now and wait. His job was to baby-sit the look-alike until further notice. Ethan would follow Jenn, listen and wait.

And pray.

This whole sting was risky. The greatest risk was to Jenn, but Ethan knew that he and Simon were taking liberties with the Colby Agency as well. If this thing went sour, Victoria could be held accountable. As he'd told Jenn, kidnapping was a felony. But Ethan trusted Jenn. She was the real Jennifer Ballard. One way or another, Ethan intended to prove it.

When he would have eased out of the small parking area and into the street to follow the dark Mercedes, fear abruptly constricted his chest.

The car nosed into a loading zone between two buildings adjacent to Ethan's position, then pulled out onto the street. They headed in the wrong direction.

A male voice echoed in Ethan's earpiece. "Madam, there's been a change of plans. Dr. Crane would like you to meet him at the residence."

*Crane was back.*

Jenn was being delivered straight to him.

# Chapter Twelve

*A change of plans?*

The blunt, completely unexpected statement chilled Jenn all the way to the bone.

David wasn't at his foundation meeting. He was waiting for her at the house. *Her home.*

"Fine," she said stiffly. "Thank you, Davenport."

The driver nodded once. Jenn squeezed her eyes shut and prayed that she could be brave enough to do this, to face David without giving herself away. Would he recognize the subtle difference between her voice and the impostor's? How was she supposed to act? Loving? Respectful? She forced herself to take several long, deep breaths. She had to be strong. She could do this.

A sudden realization brought a tiny smile to her lips. She would get to see her father. That was the one bright spot in all this. Tears brimmed behind her lashes. *Please let him be all right,* she beseeched.

Forcing herself to relax fully against the seat, she resisted the urge to turn around and look for Ethan behind her. She didn't have to worry about that. Ethan wouldn't let her down, she could count on him.

She suddenly wondered why a good-looking, incredible man like him wasn't married already. What was she thinking? He was probably one of those guys who wanted to remain a bachelor forever. But there was something about the way he'd looked at her this morning that made her feel special. It was more than the lovemaking…it was a connection she didn't quite know how to describe. A depth of emotion beyond any other she'd ever experienced. He'd touched her in a place deep inside that she hadn't known existed. She smiled, warmth rushing through her all over again at the thought of his kisses, his touch. She got the distinct impression that she touched him deep inside as well.

Her smile faded as she considered the highway stretching out before her. Would she live to enjoy whatever the future held for the two of them? Or would her life be over minutes from now?

"Was the foundation meeting canceled?" she asked the driver. There had to be some reason David had changed his plans. He was so anal-retentive, she couldn't see him deviating from the norm without some extraordinary motivation.

"No, madam," Davenport told her. "Apparently he received a telephone call that took him away from the meeting. Whatever the case, he wishes to meet with you immediately."

Fear, stark and vivid, squeezed her heart. What if something had happened to her father? She blinked, possibilities flitting through her churning mind. What if David knew about the DNA and print analysis? That she and Ethan were plotting to reveal his lies at this very moment?

An endless, nerve-wracking fifteen minutes later, Davenport angled the Mercedes into the long drive circling the front lawn of the Ballard estate. He braked to a stop directly in front of the double-doored entry that beckoned from the top of a dozen sprawling, polished granite steps.

*Home.* She'd been afraid she would never be able to set foot inside those doors ever again. As Davenport hopped out and rounded the front of the car, a mixture of fear and anticipation shrouded her. Her hands shook. She draped the purse strap over her shoulder, the shopping bag on her arm and clasped her hands together to still them.

She swallowed against the dryness in her throat and emerged slowly from the car as the door opened. The heat, unusually oppressive and thickly humid, assaulted her the moment she stepped out into the midday sun. In spite of the heat, something cold and frightening was building inside her, stealing her courage. Davenport offered her a final smile and hurried back around to the driver's side of the car.

Jenn moistened her lips and started up the steps. Covertly, she looked down. "Are you still there?" she whispered.

"Watching every move you make," Ethan's reassuring voice sounded in the tiny, flesh-colored wireless receiver she wore in the canal of her ear.

Another tiny unit was attached to the fabric of her jacket beneath the upper edge of the lapel. Ethan had explained that the unit was extremely sensitive, would pick up every sound, even in a large room. The receiving range was a great deal farther than she had expected, too. Just knowing he was there, listening, waiting to come to her rescue, made what she had to do so much easier.

At the top of the steps the door swung open. "Good afternoon, Ms. Jennifer," Carlisle, the butler who'd worked for her family for as long as she could remember, greeted.

She wanted to hug him. It was so good to see a familiar, friendly face. "How is my father?" she asked, her heart suddenly pounding all over again at the prospect of seeing him any second now.

"As well as can be expected," Carlisle told her, his tone professional, but his eyes, the expression on his face, sad in a very personal way. "We did have several moments today when I think he was actually awake, but he didn't try to speak."

Jenn could scarcely contain the tears now. "That's excellent."

Carlisle looked at her earnestly, a line furrowing his aristocratic brow. "I'm so pleased to see that you're feeling more like your old self now."

Jenn suppressed a frown, kept the smile in place. The imposter hadn't fooled everyone, not completely, anyway. "I haven't been myself," she offered, feeling the need to right whatever wrongs the other woman had committed.

A wide smile spread across the older man's face. "Well, you're feeling better now, that's what matters."

She nodded, the movement stiff, awkward. "I think I'll go up and see my father now." She hoped they hadn't moved him from his room. He had never been comfortable anywhere but in his own bed. She remembered well the numerous times they'd traveled, he'd always said there was no place on earth like his own bed.

Carlisle looked hesitant. "Of course, madam, but Dr. Crane is waiting for you in your suite."

*Their suite?* Though the house had six bedrooms, only two were suites, hers and her fathers. "I'll only be a moment," she insisted. The idea that David had moved into her bedroom sickened her.

Jenn hurried away from Carlisle's concerned eyes, her heels clicking on the marble floor. She rushed up the right side of the staircase that flowed upward on both sides of the massive entry hall. On the second-story landing, she took the right corridor and walked as fast as she could toward her father's room. The plush carpeting muffled her footsteps.

She paused outside the door to gather her composure. She had to be strong. Smile, no crying. If he was awake and aware of anything around him, she did not want to add to his misery by crying. Had he realized she'd been gone the past week? Or had the other woman put in the occasional appearance for the staff's benefit?

What had the impostor said to Jenn's father? Had she touched him? Hurt him in anyway? Fury boiled up inside her so intense she could almost taste it.

"Careful, Jenn." Ethan's husky voice whispered in her ear.

"I'm fine," she breathed as she opened the door and walked into the room.

The smell of antiseptics and sickness immediately hit her. A chill hung in the dimly lit room. A nurse sat at a desk ten or twelve feet from her father's bed. She was reading a book, but looked up as Jenn entered the room.

"Dr. Crane," the nurse said, a smile instantly slipping into place. "Your father is resting much more comfortably today. Your husband checked on him only a few minutes ago."

Jenn fought the renewed terror clawing at her insides. She hated that the nurse called her Dr. *Crane*. She hated even more that David had been in her father's room.

"Thank you for the update," Jenn said coolly, doing her best to speak more like the other woman than herself. "I'd like a moment."

The nurse nodded and stepped outside the room. Jenn prayed she wouldn't become suspicious at the request. She couldn't imagine the impostor wanting time alone with her father.

Moving quietly so as not to disturb him, Jenn abandoned the purse and shopping bag on the floor and approached her father's bed. A shaky breath slipped from her lungs as she clamped down on her lower lip to hold back the tears. He looked so frail...so deathly pale and still. She sank down on the edge of the bed and reached for his hand. His flesh was too cool and so very thin, practically every vessel was visible beneath the nearly transparent skin.

Two IV catheters were attached to his right arm, fluids and medication pumping into his veins. A feeding tube as well as an oxygen tube were in place. His breathing was shallow and a little rapid. The screen displaying his vitals showed an increased heart rate, but even with that his blood pressure was dangerously low. She shook her head. The medicine and the fluids couldn't keep him going much longer. He would die soon, she was sure of it. And no one knew the reason why. The team of specialists who'd taken his case could find nothing.

The team had suggested early on that her father might have been exposed to something they were unaware of in the lab. But Jenn had made available to them every single project her father had participated in—except Cellneu.

Another burst of fear slammed her heart against her sternum. No. It couldn't be that. Her father had never actually done any of the hands-on work with Cellneu. He'd acted more in an advisory capacity. The only way he could have been exposed was if someone deliberately...

"Oh, God," she cried softly.

"Jenn, are you all right?" Ethan demanded. "Answer me," he barked when she didn't respond right away, "or I'm blowing your cover *now*."

Jenn swiped at her eyes and took a calming breath. "It's okay," she managed to get out past the lump of emotion in her throat. "I'm heading to the suite now," she murmured.

She heard Ethan's heavy exhale. "Be careful. If this thing starts to unravel, get out. Remember, our primary objective is to get Crane to BalPhar. If that looks undoable, I want you out of there.''

She nodded, though she knew he couldn't see her. It didn't matter though. It was an order not a request. Giving her father's hand one last squeeze, she eased from the edge of the bed and started to back away, reluctant to break the touch of their hands. His eyes suddenly opened. He looked directly at Jenn.

Barely holding on to herself, she leaned forward and kissed his cheek. ''I love you, Daddy,'' she whispered near his ear.

His fingers tightened on hers. She looked deep into those blue eyes and she saw the fear there. He knew. He knew, and he was afraid for her.

Her pulse leaped. ''I'm okay. Don't worry.''

When his eyes drifted shut once more, she snagged the abandoned items on the floor, smiled for the nurse waiting outside her father's room, and headed to the east wing of the house…to the bedroom suite that she and David were supposedly sharing now.

The blood was rushing through her body, pounding in her head. The horrifying images from the chapel replayed in her mind as she made the journey to where David waited. She hesitated outside the door. Checked her suit, swiped her eyes and took a steadying breath.

*Show time,* she told herself silently.

In that infinitesimal moment as she reached for the doorknob, she recalled every second she'd spent in Ethan's arms. The way he'd protected her…the way he'd made love to her and suddenly she knew what all the mixed-up emotions inside her meant.

"I love you, Ethan," she whispered so softly she doubted he would hear her, then she opened the door.

"Darling, I've been waiting," David announced as he poured a second glass of champagne.

The shopping bag and purse slipped unhampered to the floor. One second turned to five as she stared at the man who had professed his love for her...who'd asked her to be his wife and then tried to kill her. He looked exactly the same as before. It seemed strange now that she could ever have considered him kind and compassionate. But looks could be deceiving. She knew that all too well now. David was the epitome of deception and yet, outwardly, he appeared so normal. A man of distinction, attractive, even. Well-bred and even better dressed.

But he was evil inside.

Evil and deadly.

Knowing that her father was hanging on had given her the strength and courage to do what she knew had to be done.

"Sorry to keep you waiting," she said without even realizing she'd intended to. "I had a stop to make." She even smiled, falling right into her part.

He crossed the room, the two stemmed glasses in his hands. "Oh, trust me, darling, it was worth the wait."

He offered her one of the glasses, she accepted. The fact that her hand didn't shake was nothing short of a miracle. "Are we celebrating something?" she asked, then sipped the bubbly more for courage than to dampen her dry throat.

"Oh, yes." He leaned down and kissed her cheek.

It took every ounce of willpower in her body not to stiffen and draw away from his touch.

"We have the world to celebrate," he enthused, then clinked their glasses. "To overcoming the FDA's final hurdle." He smiled widely. "And to Cellneu."

Ethan didn't have to see Jenn to know how that announcement affected her. Time was truly the enemy now. They had to move even more quickly. Getting Jenn out of that house and to BalPhar was top priority. She could only get the evidence they needed at BalPhar. And Ethan didn't want her alone in that room with Crane any longer than was necessary. The idea that he was touching her, had kissed her, seared through Ethan with such fury and force that he had to clench the steering wheel to keep from bolting from the vehicle.

*I love you, Ethan,* was still ringing in his ears. Part of him reeled with emotion at the possibility, but another part of him, a saner part, reasoned that she was only reacting to the stress. She couldn't possibly love him. They'd only been together a few days…had only made love that morning. He'd protected her and she was feeling grateful, that's all. That little voice that nagged at him about his own feelings tried to rally above all else, but Ethan squashed it.

He had to focus now. Jenn's whole life hinged on the next few minutes.

"Why don't you get comfortable, darling," Crane suggested, his tone low, what he considered seductive.

Ethan tensed. He'd thought every muscle in his body was already on edge, but the tension cranked up another notch.

"Just one more toast," Jenn suggested, her voice sounded provocative, but Ethan heard the underlying fear there.

He gritted his teeth against the anxiety rocketing inside him. He had to get her out of the house. *Now.* But how? He doubted anything short of a fire would tear Crane away. He didn't dare say anything to Jenn that might distract her.

The sound of champagne spilling into a glass echoed in his ears.

"I hope you're wearing that new black teddy I bought you," Crane said wolfishly.

Ethan muted his mike. He swore profusely as his mind scrambled for some way to get her out of there. He had to act fast. The answer hit him like a sledgehammer between the eyes.

He quickly punched in the number for BalPhar's main operator. Blood roared in his ears as he waited for the operator to answer.

"Ballard Pharmaceuticals," a crisp professional voice intoned.

He didn't even bother to disguise his voice. "You have one hour to evacuate the facility or they will all die. You'll never find the explosives in time."

He disconnected the call, then reset the volume on his mike.

All he could do now was hope.

Or blow Jenn's cover if the call didn't get the reaction he hoped for fast enough.

"Mmmmm...you taste different," Crane murmured. "Are you wearing a new kind of perfume or lotion?"

"A new bath oil," Jenn responded quickly. Her voice was too shrill.

Ethan swore. Dammit, she was going to give herself away if she didn't stay calm. He closed his eyes and fought the images of what was likely taking place. Crane touching her...kissing her...tasting her skin. Ethan wanted to kill him with his bare hands.

"David," Jenn protested, "let me get undressed first."

"Enough!" Ethan bolted from the SUV, simultaneously drawing his gun. "I'm coming in."

What sounded like a knock reverberated in his earpiece.

Silence.

Door opening.

"Yes, what is it?"

"I'm sorry, sir, but it's your secretary," another male voice, a decidedly distinguished one, said. *The butler.* "She claims it's urgent, sir. The call is on line one."

Ethan halted abruptly. "Standing down for the moment," he murmured to Jenn, then listened for Crane's reaction to the call.

"Thank you, Carlisle."

A door closed.

Ethan eased back into the concealing bushes. He struggled to slow his respiration. Calm and focused, he had to be both.

A glass thumped lightly on a table. "Yes, Renée, what is it?" Crane sounded annoyed, frustrated.

Ethan was overjoyed.

"You're joking?" Crane demanded.

Silence.

"I'll be right there."

The sound of the phone clattering into its cradle.

"Is something wrong?" Jenn asked.

*Only the tremor in your voice,* Ethan wanted to say, but wouldn't. Even the slightest change in her facial expression might be noticed.

"We may have to evacuate the facility, there's been a bomb threat," Crane answered, distracted, concerned. "I have to go out there and find out what's going on. Extremists may have discovered how close we are to testing Cellneu on humans."

"I'm going with you."

Silence.

Ethan held his breath.

More silence.

"All right. I may need your help."

Ethan slipped back into his SUV as he listened to Jenn and Crane rush to leave the house. The black Mercedes had already pulled around to the front by the time they walked out the door.

Using his binoculars, Ethan watched Crane as he escorted Jenn down the steps and to the car with a hand on her elbow. He was thankful that she didn't glance in his direction before getting into the waiting car. Ethan exhaled, relieved that she hadn't stumbled even once.

"We'll have to pick up where we left off a little later," Crane suggested.

Jenn giggled in response, the same sultry, bubbly laughter she'd heard the impostor utter while Simon charmed her. It was perfect. Ethan was immensely proud of her.

And still scared to death.

If anything happened to her...

Once the Mercedes had disappeared in the distance, Ethan eased out onto the service road and followed.

"I'm right behind you," he said softly. "You're doing great."

It would take twenty minutes to reach the facility. Security was probably already searching every nook and cranny. It wouldn't take long to discover the call was a crank. But certain steps would be taken just the same. Surely not even David Crane would risk the welfare of all those in his employ. Then again, he just might.

The next thing Ethan heard was a confirmation of that very thought.

Crane had called someone on his cell phone. "Let's keep this low-key. Don't evacuate the priority labs until we have absolute proof the threat is legitimate. This wouldn't be the first time we've been the butt of someone's idea of a joke."

Crane sounded angry now.

"Good," he said after a pause. "Still no trace of her? I want her and Delaney both found. They're close. I can feel it."

Ethan almost laughed at that one. If the guy only knew how close.

Ethan waited a full five minutes after the Mercedes cleared the gate before he approached. He'd pulled on a ball cap and gotten his ID ready, then muted his mike once more.

Ethan stopped at the gate and waited for the guard to saunter out of his office. He carried a clipboard.

"Name?" he asked.

Ethan nodded a greeting to him. "You won't find my name on that list," he said coolly.

The guard shrugged. "If you're not on the list, you won't be going in," he said smugly.

Ethan fixed him with his most lethal stare. The one that would stop a charging bull in its tracks. He flashed his fake ID, which looked both official and authoritative. "We don't have time to exchange pleasantries," he snapped. "My name is Barclay. I'm a demolitions expert. I don't know if you're aware of this or not, but a bomb threat has been called into this facility. I'm here to assist in controlling the threat."

The guy's eyes rounded. "I'll...I'll have to check that with the chief. I don't know anything about a bomb threat."

Ethan looked at his wristwatch. "I have twenty-nine minutes left to defuse the explosives. Doctor Crane asked me to follow him in." He glanced at the guy's nametag. *"Bob."*

Bob's eyes bulged this time. "You mean there really is a bomb in there?"

"We're wasting valuable time," Ethan barked. Obviously little or nothing had been done to usher employees to safety.

The guy nodded. "Okay, okay. I'll let you in. Dr. Crane just went in. Is anyone else coming to help you?" he asked, his head still jerking up and down.

"I was in the area so I came ahead," Ethan assured

him. "The rest of the team will be here any minute," he suggested.

"I'll open the gate," Bob shouted over his shoulder.

When the impressive-looking gates swung open, Ethan drove through and searched for a parking spot near the west exit, the one he planned to use to get inside when the time came.

"I'll wait here for you," Jenn said.

Ethan almost jumped after the long minutes of silence. Jenn hadn't spoken since they arrived at the facility. If Crane had, he'd moved out of range of the mike she wore.

"Renèe will get you anything you need," Crane said. He must have walked out then because Ethan heard a door close.

"I'm in," Jenn murmured.

"Okay," Ethan said tightly.

She was in Crane's office. All she had to do now was find the evidence they needed.

# *Chapter Thirteen*

Jenn had decided that if David had kept any of Kessler's records indicating Cellneu had problems, they would be in his private office.

And she was nearly certain he would have kept something. It was the oldest cover-your-behind trick in the book. This way when problems showed up later, David could provide new evidence, evidence he'd supposedly just found, to show that Kessler or her father had hidden the problems. BalPhar would be damaged beyond repair, but David would come out smelling like a rose. He'd squirrel away all the riches from Cellneu in a Swiss bank account. Then, when the proverbial crap hit the fan, the company would file bankruptcy.

He'd thought of everything, she'd bet. David wouldn't take any chances. But she was going to make sure he failed. She would not allow him to hurt all the people who would believe that Cellneu was the answer to their prayers. Nor would she allow him to destroy her father's life's work.

"Find anything yet?"

Ethan's voice sounded in her earpiece, at once reassuring and arousing. Though he waited in the SUV, the mere sound of his deep voice made her feel all warm and tingly inside.

"No," she whispered, trying to force her thoughts back to the task at hand. This was definitely not the time to be thinking about sex and the man she loved.

Her fingers stilled mid-search in the bottom file drawer of David's credenza. She did love Ethan. She'd told him so. She hadn't actually meant to, but fear that she might never see him again had spurred her on. So she'd told him.

She hurried through the remaining folders in that drawer, then opened the top one on the opposite end. "I meant what I said, you know," she murmured, fishing for a reaction.

She heard his soft sigh. She tried not to consider it a negative response as she scanned the neatly printed labels on each folder.

"We'll talk about that when you're out of there," he said, skirting the issue altogether.

Well, at least he hadn't said she was nuts, which she probably was.

But she loved him anyway. She smiled as she turned back to the desk and considered how she would get those drawers open. She was in love, all right. Though she wasn't a virgin anymore, she definitely intended to marry the man who'd deflowered her. He just didn't know it yet. Her smile stretched to a grin. She wasn't worried, she'd talk him into it. Look at all she'd talked him into so far.

She searched the top of the desk and any drawer that

would open, no keys, no trip levers. Nothing she attempted freed the two locked file drawers in Crane's desk. "I can't get the file drawers in his desk to open and there's no key." Searching his computer would be useless. Without his PIN, she'd never get into his system.

"Do each of the drawers have a lock?"

She looked left, then right. "Yes, and they look like the same type of lock."

"Is there a letter opener on his desk?"

Jenn pushed to her feet and scanned the desktop. Silver blade, mahogany handle. "Got it."

"Insert the tip in the lock as far as you can and twist it, jiggle it, whatever. You should be able to work the lock loose. Those kind usually aren't very reliable."

"I'll try." She dropped back into a crouch.

As Jenn worked, she considered that she'd survived explosions, fired a weapon, almost drowned, been instrumental in causing a car crash, helped steal another car, been shot at, stolen files from BalPhar, helped kidnap a woman, impersonated the person impersonating her and now she was breaking into David's personal files.

She was a criminal!

That's better than being dead, she mused.

And that didn't even take into consideration that she'd fallen in love and lost her virginity in the middle of it all. Sheesh, she'd been a busy girl.

The first lock gave way. Jenn jerked the drawer open. "Voilà," she said to Ethan.

"Good girl."

Her hackles rose. "If you don't know by now that I'm not a little girl…" she sassed.

Another little sigh. "Sorry about that. Temporary lapse."

She harrumphed as she fingered through the files. Nothing of interest. Defeat started to nag at her. What if he'd already destroyed everything? But that didn't make sense. He'd need something to cover his butt.

The next lock was much easier. Jenn knew just how to twist the letter opener. By the time she'd flipped through half the folders, her hopes had plummeted even lower.

"It's not here," she whispered. But where else would it be? David would never risk leaving that file where someone else might stumble upon them. He was too clever for that.

"If you can't find it, just get out," Ethan ordered. She was pretty sure she heard worry in his voice. "You've been in there ten minutes already. He could come back anytime."

Suddenly there it was!

The next label she read was: Cellneu.

She jerked the folder from the drawer, going back on her haunches. Reports, memos, handwritten notes from Kessler. All of which warned against the use of Cellneu. New discoveries, Kessler annotated, proved that genetic alternations to non-cancerous cells occurred. These new, altered cells would eventually wreak so much damage that the testing specimen would die. The notes were dated more than a year ago.

"God," Jenn murmured.

"Did you find something?" Ethan wanted to know.

"I've got it." Adrenaline surged through her veins. She had the proof in her hands.

"Then get out of there," Ethan commanded.

Jenn shuffled the papers back into the folder. She reached beneath her jacket and tucked it into the waistband of her skirt just in case she ran into anyone on the way out. As she was closing the drawer something else caught her eye.

Jennifer Ballard.

Though her mind was screaming for her to leave, she couldn't. She simply couldn't move without seeing what was in that file. The one with her name on it.

She opened the folder and scanned the contents. A number of the documents were dated before she was born. The more she read, the more her mind raced, only now in a different direction. All thoughts of walking out of the building had evacuated her brain. She could only read the details so clearly documented before her.

"What are you doing?" Ethan demanded. "Get out of there."

She shook her head, too absorbed to speak.

The door suddenly opened.

"It was nothing but—"

She looked up.

David stopped cold, his mouth hanging open.

Jenn slowly rose to her feet, the file with her name on it in her hands. "What is this?"

"Dammit, Jenn, get out of there!" Ethan roared in her ear. She heard the slamming of the SUV door; he'd gotten out. He was coming in.

She ignored him.

"This file." She gestured toward David with the folder. "What is all this stuff?"

"How the hell did *you*—" He caught himself before he finished. "Where is—"

Jenn cocked an eyebrow. "Your little friend who looks so much like me?" she deadpanned.

David suddenly smiled, all signs of surprise cleared from his face as he strolled across the room. "Thank you for saving me the trouble of tracking you down. Where's your big, bad protector?"

Jenn started to speak, but Ethan's voice interrupted her. "You tell that son of a bitch I'm on my way and that when I get there, I'm going to kill him."

Jenn wasn't going there. "Maybe I'd better tell you where your friend is first."

"Do tell." David paused on the opposite side of the desk. He reached into his jacket pocket and produced his cell phone. "Just give me one moment," he said politely as he punched in someone's number. "Get up here," he growled. "And put security on alert. Ethan Delaney is probably around here somewhere. Who? Why wasn't I informed? I didn't call in any demolitions expert!"

Jenn struggled to stay calm, to keep her limbs steady. She had to make him believe that she wasn't afraid, that she had a plan…evidence.

"I'm sorry," David placated. "You were saying?" He dropped the phone back into his pocket.

"Your friend," Jenn repeated, "she's with a homicide detective right now telling him everything she knows about you. That you killed Russ, Kessler and that Cellneu is a sham.''

David propped a hip on the edge of the desk. Jenn held her ground. She didn't cower.

"Really? That's interesting.'' He looked deep into her eyes. "But I know you're lying. You never were very good at it. Besides, Pamela would never betray me. Without me she gets nothing.''

Jenn shrugged with feigned indifference. "Maybe you're right. Maybe she won't give you up. She might just take the rap herself. That part really doesn't matter to me. With Kessler's files, we have all we need to stop Cellneu.''

"Then why come here?'' he inquired smugly. "For old time's sake?''

He stood, skirted the desk and moved slowly in her direction. She was afraid now. Really afraid. She couldn't stop the quaking in her limbs no matter how hard she tried. He stopped only a couple of feet away, looming over her.

She lifted her chin and glared up at him. "I just wanted to see if I could fool you. And I did.''

He laughed, an evil, menacing sound. "Yes. You did fool me for just a little while.'' He trailed a finger down her arm. "But you see, Pamela isn't frigid like you. I would definitely have known the difference.''

She jerked away from his touch. "Like I'd let you near me.''

Fury blazed in his eyes. "I understand that you haven't avoided Delaney's arms,'' he spat.

Jenn smiled triumphantly though she wondered

vaguely how he could know that. It had to be a calculated guess. "Definitely not. I gave him what you'll never have."

David manacled her arms, his fingers like steel bands biting into her skin. "Do you think I care? I have what I want. I have everything. I even own your existence."

"What is all this?" she demanded, determined to have her answer about the file even if she died immediately afterwards.

He shoved her away. She stumbled, caught herself before she hit the floor.

"It's the Ballard family's dirty little secret," he snarled. "All this time you'd thought you were daddy's perfect little girl, that he was the perfect father, that your whole life was just perfect."

He moved his head slowly from left to right. "But it's all built on a lie."

She threw the folder at him. It banked off his chest and the contents scattered on the floor. "Nothing you can say will make me believe you," she shouted, tears welling in her eyes.

"Well let's just see, shall we?" He took an intimidating step nearer, closing the distance between them yet again. "Let's start with your lovely mother."

Jenn wanted to put her hands over her ears to block out his words but she couldn't move. She could only stand there and peer into those diabolical eyes.

Three men rushed into the office. David glanced briefly in their direction. "Wait outside," he snapped. "Keep your eyes open for Delaney."

Jenn remained paralyzed. She wanted to call out to

the men, to tell them the truth about their employer, but she was helpless to do anything but listen to his horrible words as he turned toward her once more.

"Your mother couldn't conceive. Nothing worked. So you were a test-tube baby."

Jenn summoned a smidgen of courage. "So what? It's not like it was anything new at that point." In vitro fertilization had started years before she was born. Lots of couples went that route, still did.

"Ah, but your case was a bit different," he told her with obvious glee. "Your zygote split. Identical twins." He waved his hands with a flourish to punctuate his words and took yet another step in her direction.

Jenn felt suddenly sick to her stomach. The other woman was her twin sister? That just wasn't possible. Her father would have told her something that important. This was insane. David had obviously lost his mind. Her gaze drifted down to the papers on the floor. But there was documentation. She'd looked at part of it.

"*Daddy* was just thrilled with that new development," David went on, his tone so disgustingly smug. "In fact, he was so thrilled, he decided to play God for a day."

Jenn shook her head. "You're insane. My father would never do that."

David angled his head and reveled in her pain. He reached out and traced her cheek. She shuddered.

"Oh, but he did. Daddy decided to alter one embryo. He wanted to see if he could create a genius." David wiggled his eyebrows. "And the rest is history."

Jenn had been called a genius since she was four years old. But both her mother and father were extremely intelligent. It wasn't outside the realm of possibility that she would be bright as well. David's story was just too bizarre. He was trying to hurt her. That's all it could be.

"If all you say is true, then why was I never told about my twin?" she demanded.

"That's an easy one."

He'd backed her up against the desk. There was nowhere for her to run. Her heart stuttered.

"Your father didn't know your sister survived."

Jenn's expression narrowed. "How is that possible?"

"Dear old Uncle Russ decided that what your father had done was wrong. So he took matters into his own hands. He feared that if your father was successful there might be no end to the genetic alterations he would attempt in the future. Russ made sure that only one of you survived—at least as far as the world, including your father, knew." David kicked some of the papers on the floor aside and moved another step closer to her. "Your father never even knew the other embryo survived. Feeling guilty for what he'd done, Russ made sure the other embryo was safely implanted in another host."

This couldn't be true. "I don't believe you." The fingers of her right hand gripped the edge of the desk. Could she propel herself around the corner of the desk before he moved closer, trapping her completely?

David gestured to the mass of papers on the floor.

"It's all there. I'm sorry you won't have time to read all the fascinating details."

She shook her head in denial. "If this is true, how did you find out?"

"That's the really amazing part," he crooned. "Your father told me."

"You said he didn't know," she argued.

"He didn't. Not until Russ told him six months ago, anyway."

"Why would Russ tell him after all these years?" She didn't want to believe any of it. But she'd seen part of the papers. She'd seen the other woman. The prints and DNA matched. At least part of it was fact.

"When your father's health went to hell, Russ began to feel guilty. Thought he ought to know the truth, so he told him. Since your father realized how very much I loved you," he added saccharinely, "he asked me to find the twin and give him a full report on what her life was like. When I first found her, I was amazed. She was an exact double. Not educated or refined like you, but otherwise, a perfect duplicate."

"How did you find her?" Jenn's heart was thundering now. She didn't want to hear anymore, but she had to. She had to know all of it.

"Russ knew where she was. Had all along. When I told your father that she was working in New Orleans and doing fine after being raised by a fine Indiana family, he seemed satisfied."

"Why didn't he tell me?" she asked, her voice hollow. The hurt she suddenly felt drained the last of the fight from her.

"Oh, you know what a martyr he is. He didn't want to disrupt either of your lives. Especially since I assured him that your twin had a wonderful life."

"You lied." Jenn suddenly had a horrible feeling about the rest.

"Of course, I lied." He laughed. "It was easy from there. I'd marry you, get rid of your father, then I'd get rid of you. Pamela was only too happy to take your place in the lap of luxury. After the pathetic way she'd grown up, she decided that she had it coming to her."

His face darkened. "It would have worked, too, if Russ hadn't discovered what I'd hidden about Cellneu. Then my whole plan went to hell. But now everything is under control again. You're dead and your father will be too before the night is through."

Enlightenment struck her. "What did you do to my father? You made him sick!" Dear God, it was true. This man she'd planned to marry, thought she really cared about, was killing her father. Quite possibly already had.

"That was a stroke of pure genius. I knew just what kind of drugs to administer to get the right effect and no one would ever find it."

"Cellneu?" she had to know.

"Oh, no. I wouldn't risk Cellneu. It's my own personal blend. A steady dosage in his IV has the desired effect. Tonight that dosage is going to be tripled. Goodbye, Daddy. I'm sure Pamela will be devastated."

A sudden burst of fear combined with anger gave Jenn the courage to scoot slightly away from him. She couldn't let that happen. She had to save her father. "I won't let you do this."

David shouted for his men waiting outside the door. "Too bad there's nothing you can do. Like I said, you're dead."

ETHAN BURST from the stairwell onto the tenth floor. He didn't risk taking the elevator in case he was spotted and security shut down the power to the shaft. He'd already called Simon for backup. He'd be here soon since he was on standby. Ethan knew good backup was the key to any operation. Amy Wells was staying with the impostor. Pamela, according to Crane.

Running hard, Ethan didn't stop when he reached Crane's secretary's office. He jumped onto her desk then propelled himself from that elevated position, landing smack in the middle of three security guards postured to storm Crane's office. Weapons fired. One man went down.

Crane's voice squalled in Ethan's earpiece again. He called out to his guards again. But they were a little busy, Ethan thought, as he landed a good right hook.

"Ethan!"

Jenn's voice. A scream.

Ethan intensified his efforts. The struggle continued for about three more seconds. A second guard went down. Then the last. One was dead, the remaining two only disabled.

He lunged for the door to Crane's office.

"I don't have a problem simply killing you myself," Crane growled.

"Ethan! He's got a gun!"

His heart hammering in his chest, Ethan grabbed for the doorknob.

"Halt or I'll shoot!" A voice behind him demanded.

Ethan didn't stop.

# Chapter Fourteen

Ethan hurled himself through the door, diving for the floor, rolling, then rising to a shooting crouch. The security guard behind him fired again, the shot going wide just like the first one. Ethan wondered briefly where the hell these guys learned to shoot. He pivoted and shot the guard high in the right shoulder. He went down like a rock. He wasn't dead, but he wasn't going to do any more shooting either. Ethan spun back in Crane's direction, he took a bead right between the bastard's eyes.

Standing next to his desk, Crane held Jenn in front of him like a shield, a small-caliber handgun pressed against her temple.

"Drop your weapon, Crane, and I'll let you live," Ethan ordered. He kept his gaze focused carefully on Crane. If he looked at Jenn, really looked at her, he would lose it. He could already feel the panic churning in his gut.

"Come now, Ethan, you don't really expect me to do something so stupid, do you?" Crane laughed. "I wasn't even that naive ten years ago."

A flash from the past whizzed across Ethan's line of

vision. He blinked it away and refocused on his target. The fact that Crane had saved his life didn't matter now. He'd evened that score long ago. He clenched his jaw against the doubt. This was not the same man he'd known ten years ago.

David Crane was a cheat and a murderer. After what he'd done to Jenn and her father, he didn't deserve to live.

Crane smiled, the expression sinister. "It's so easy to read you, my dear friend. You're weighing all the reasons you should kill me." He yanked Jenn to him. "Tell me, is she worth killing me for? Because the only way you're getting her back is by killing me. Can you live with that, Ethan?" He cocked his head toward his shoulder in a shrug. "Then again, I might take her to hell with me just to piss you off."

Ethan could hear a stampede of footsteps in the corridor outside the secretary's office. Any second now they'd be overrun by BalPhar security. Men who reported to David Crane.

"Let her go," Ethan said, slowly rising to his feet. "Let her go and use me as your ticket out of here." He flared his free hand. "It's your only way out now."

"It's true," Jenn put in quickly, her voice shaky. "I'm wearing a wire. Everything you've said has been taped by another Colby agent."

Smooth move, Ethan mused. He looked directly at Jenn for the first time since entering the room. She looked terrified, but amazingly brave and absolutely beautiful. He wanted to hold her and tell her what a great job she'd done. He forced his gaze back to Crane's.

"I'll put my weapon down and we'll walk out of here before the authorities arrive."

Not that the authorities had even been called, but Crane had no way of knowing that.

Crane shook his head. "The bomb threat was you," he said as if the epiphany had just that second struck him. "You crafty bastard. That's how you got me here." His fingers tangled in Jenn's hair and jerked her head back. "How you got her here."

"Give the guy a cigar," Ethan smirked. "You just figuring all that out? A little slow on the uptake today, aren't we?"

Crane's expression hardened, his eyes glazed with fury. "I'm going to kill her," he snarled. "I consider it my obligation to make sure you're entertained."

"You want her dead more than you want out of here?" Ethan moved forward a step. "Are you sure about that?"

Crane faltered. "Put your gun down first."

Ethan pretended to consider the suggestion. "All right." Crane didn't know about the ankle holster either. "We'll do it together. I lay my gun down, you release her."

Crane nodded. "Come closer. I want this to be up close and personal."

Ethan eased closer. All he needed was a clear head shot and Crane would be out of the picture.

"Now," Crane said when Ethan was three or four

feet away. "Put your weapon down on the desk and put your hands up."

Like that was going to happen in this lifetime. Ethan glanced at Jenn as he started to lower his weapon. The panic in her eyes sent warning bells off in his head. Dammit. She didn't understand that he wasn't going to let Crane have the upper hand.

The whole scene seemed to lapse into slow motion as Crane relaxed his hold on her ever so slightly. Ethan's arm came back up. Jenn grabbed the letter opener from the desk.

Crane's eyes widened as he realized Ethan wasn't putting the weapon down. Jenn stabbed Crane in the thigh, the letter opener sinking to the hilt.

Shock registered in Crane's eyes at the same instant that the weapon in his hand came up a notch.

"Get down!" Ethan roared to Jenn.

Jenn jerked free.

Crane fired.

Ethan fired.

The loud reports echoed in the room.

Crane jerked back.

Jenn hit the floor.

Silence.

Ethan's gaze went immediately to her.

She cautiously looked up from the heap she'd made on the floor.

Thank God. "Are you all right?" he asked, his voice as shaky as hers had been just minutes ago.

She nodded, then looked over her shoulder.

"He's dead," Ethan assured her. He lowered his

weapon, relief gushing through him, making him weak. He started toward her—

The sound of weapons engaging echoed in the room.

Ethan jerked his head in the direction of the sound. Six more security guards poured through the door. The one on the floor suddenly started screaming bloody murder.

"Drop the weapon," the one who appeared to be in charge demanded.

Ethan had known they were coming. He'd heard them. He just hadn't expected them to make it this far. Simon should have been here by now.

"Joe," Jenn said, clearly recognizing the man. "Thank goodness you're here."

"Dr. Crane, are you all right?" the guard she'd called Joe asked. He looked from Ethan to her and back.

Though Ethan had lowered his weapon, he didn't drop it. He wouldn't until he had no other choice.

"I'm fine." She pointed to Ethan. "This man saved my life. David Crane was a traitor."

Joe didn't look convinced. "Are you sure you're all right, Dr. Crane?"

"Please," she pleaded wearily. "Put your weapons down. He's on our side."

Joe shook his head. "Can't do that, ma'am, until he does." He nodded in Ethan's direction. "I have to subdue him."

"Unfortunately, gentlemen, that isn't going to happen."

Simon Ruhl stood behind the men, his weapon now pressed against the back of Joe's skull.

"You take the scenic route or what?" Ethan complained.

Simon sent a smile Ethan's way. "I met with a little resistance." He lifted an eyebrow then. "A fellow named Bob. Apparently someone told him there was a bomb in here."

"Oops," Ethan confessed. He was sure Bob would not soon forget meeting Simon Ruhl.

"Lower your weapons," Simon ordered the man currently feeling the brunt of his irritation.

Admitting defeat, Joe placed his weapon on the floor and kicked it a few feet away. The other guards followed suit.

Jenn rushed into Ethan's arms. "God, I thought we were both dead." She shivered against his chest.

He pressed a kiss to her hair. "You're safe now, Jenn." She drew back and looked into his eyes. "You've got your life back."

Her exuberant expression fell. "My father. I have to get back to the house. David is killing him."

Ethan rushed from the room, Jenn in tow, leaving Simon to take care of the final details.

Jenn was right. Crane was dead, but he was still killing her father.

AT HOME, Jenn sat next to her father's bed. He'd spent two weeks in the hospital, the final week under extreme protest, but he was going to recover, not fully, but close. They'd found the drugs in the IV bag that David had been using to slowly end her father's life. Fortunately, very little of the damage was permanent, but if David hadn't been stopped it would have proved fatal. Her father's excellent physical condition and savage will to live had played a major part in his fighting the drug as long as he had.

It would be months before he completely regained his strength, but it would come. That's all that mattered.

Ethan had called several times. He was back to being Ethan Delaney, Colby Agency investigator. He'd kept their conversations on a strictly platonic, mostly professional level. Jenn's heart ached each time she thought of him. Obviously their time together had not affected him the way it had her. Of course, he hadn't been the one to say the L-word. He hadn't brought up the fact that she'd said it either.

She wiped the tears from her eyes with a tissue and sucked in a deep breath. She'd survived Crane, she could survive this.

Couldn't she?

That little voice deep inside her wasn't so sure.

She loved Ethan.

Wanted to be with him more than she wanted anything in the world. She looked at her father and smiled, well more than almost anything else. His cheeks were ruddy again, his appetite strong. She was so thankful to Ethan and Victoria Colby for what they'd done to help her.

No amount of money would ever be thanks enough.

Her father's eyes opened. He blinked a couple of times, then turned to find her sitting in his favorite chair beside his bed. She smiled warmly.

"How are you feeling today?"

Talking had been pretty much forbidden the last couple of weeks. It had been imperative that every shred of his strength be used to recover. Jenn had forced herself to put off any discussion of the past or David...or Russ and Kessler. And God, of her twin Pamela.

"Well," her father whispered. "Glad to be alive." He swallowed. His eyes misted. "Very thankful that you're safe now."

"Let me get you some water." She poured some water from the pitcher into his cup and inserted a bendable straw. "Here." She placed the straw against his lips. "Sip it slowly."

He sipped once, again, then shook his head.

"There are things I want to tell you."

"Daddy, we can talk later. You have to concentrate on getting well now. Doctor's orders." She grinned for him and set the cup aside.

"I didn't know," he murmured sadly. "Russ didn't tell me until—"

"I know," Jenn cut him off gently. "David told me everything. None of this was your fault. It was David's. He used us all."

Her father blinked. "What about...her?"

Jenn took his hand in hers. "We'll talk about that later. You're not well enough right now to worry about any of this. Everything is back to normal. We'll work out that one detail later."

She wasn't about to let anything or anyone interfere with her father's recovery.

Her father nodded. "I'm so sorry."

Jenn kissed his hand. "It's not your fault. Sleep now."

Within minutes he had fallen back into a deep sleep. Jenn carefully placed his hand back on the cool sheet, then kissed his cheek. She should leave him for a while. If he woke again he'd only want to try to talk some more. He didn't need to overextend himself.

She crossed the room, smiling at the nurse as she went. Jenn had hired this one herself. She slipped out of the room, closing the door quietly behind her.

She was tired, probably needed some rest herself. She sat up far too often into the wee hours of the morning watching her father. Though she knew the nurses to be competent, Jenn was so afraid of losing him.

Losing Russ and Ethan had been tough enough. She couldn't lose the only other person on earth she had left.

Forcing her attention to other things, she descended the stairs in search of Carlisle. She needed someone to talk to. Her mind just wouldn't shut down long enough for her to sleep. It was the same thing every day, every night. She walked the floors or sat by her father's side until she was too exhausted to hold her head up any longer. Then she stumbled to the bed.

As she descended the last tread, the doorbell rang. Frowning she started to the door.

"Would you like me to get that, madam?"

She smiled at the ever-faithful Carlisle. "That's all right. I'll get it."

Carlisle disappeared back down the hall.

Jenn opened the door. Belatedly she considered that

she should have looked outside to see who was there first. But old habits die hard. She'd never realized how vulnerable a person could be until a few weeks ago.

"Hello, Jenn."

It was Ethan.

A weight lifted from her chest and all that was good in the universe suddenly filled her, sending a smile to her lips that reached all the way to her eyes.

"Ethan." She chewed her lower lip and refrained from throwing her arms around him or putting too much stock in his presence. He was probably just in the area and wanted to check on her father. Victoria most likely sent him.

He smiled back at her and her heart melted. Her entire being wept with the need to hold him again.

"I thought I'd drop by and see if you needed anything," he said, his words clearly chosen with care.

Her smile faded a little. As did her hopes. "Everything's fine. My father is recovering rapidly, and I'm…" She sighed. "Well, I'm very busy with pulling things back together at BalPhar."

He nodded. "I'm glad to hear it. They've set a trial date for Pamela."

Jenn swallowed back the emotion that instantly tried to rise in her throat. "I'm glad." At least she tried to be. She didn't want to think about how the woman probably blamed all that she'd become on what Russ and Jenn's father had done. Though Jenn sympathized with her to an extent, the lengths she'd gone to for revenge were unforgivable.

"Have you spoken to her yet?" Ethan asked quietly.

Jenn shook her head. "Maybe someday, but right now I just can't do it."

"I understand. There's a lot of hurt there. Maybe when it's healed a bit the two of you can have some sort of closure."

An awkward silence followed.

Jenn blushed. "I'm sorry." She opened the door wider. "Would you like to come in?"

He searched her eyes for a moment, his unreadable. "Actually I was hoping you'd take a walk with me."

"I'd lov—be happy to."

God, she'd almost said the L-word again.

*Calm, Jenn. Composed. Don't make a fool of yourself.*

She stepped outside and closed the door behind her. "Would you like to see the garden?"

"I'd love it," Ethan said with quiet enthusiasm.

There was something intense in those dark eyes. She smiled. And he'd said the L-word.

They walked for a while with Jenn explaining the variety of roses and other flowering shrubs the gardener tended with such care. Ethan seemed genuinely interested in every word that rambled from her overly active mouth.

She sounded like a complete idiot.

She studied him as they walked. He was so handsome. So damned perfectly made. She loved everything about him. She loved even more the way he'd protected her, tugged her across that murky river, shielded her from would-be murderers. He was a real hero. The kind one read about in paperback novels.

The kind of man who came along only once in a lifetime, and only then if a woman was really, really lucky.

She couldn't possibly let him get away.

"By the way," she said struggling to keep her tone light. "I wanted to thank the Colby Agency again for straightening out BalPhar's security. I'm not sure I would have known where to begin."

Victoria had sent in a team, including the enigmatic Simon Ruhl, a very energetic Ric Martinez and the charismatic Ian Michaels. Jenn couldn't help wondering where Victoria got all that good-looking male material. The only one she'd missed meeting was Max. Jenn felt as if she knew him already after spending so much time in his cabin.

"The Colby Agency was happy to help," Ethan said, that sexy voice only adding another layer of tension to her already off-the-chart desire. "If there's anything else you need, just let us know."

She knew what she had to do. "There is one more thing you can do for me, Ethan."

He paused, looked deeply into her eyes. "Anything. Name it."

She tried to decipher the emotion that flickered briefly in his eyes, but couldn't quite manage. "This way," she said struggling to take her eyes off his.

She led him to the gardener's shed, a plan unfolding like a map inside her head. It was almost August and the humidity level was still hovering around ninety percent, but that wasn't going to stop her.

Shadows loomed inside the shed. The temperature was a good ten degrees cooler, but still stifling.

She closed the door behind them, pitching them into semi-darkness. Tree-shaded windows at the far end of the shed allowed some light.

Ethan turned to her. "What do you want me to do?"

There was no mistaking the hunger in his eyes, the desire thickening his voice. Heat surged through Jenn, pooling between her thighs in that special place only he had touched.

"Take your clothes off," she ordered succinctly.

"I can definitely do that." A ghost of a smile kicked up one corner of his mouth as he slowly, too damned slowly, unbuttoned his shirt. His eyes never leaving hers, he peeled it away from his shoulders. Jenn's heart thumped madly. Seeing that magnificent chest always had that effect on her. Leather hissed against denim as he pulled his belt from his jeans in one long stroke. He kicked off his boots, bent down and rolled off his socks. Jenn was captivated by the shifting motion of well-defined muscle.

The unmistakable sound of his zipper being lowered jerked her gaze back to his. Her next breath trapped in her lungs. The heat in those dark, coppery eyes made her weak with want.

"I want you to make love to me, Ethan," she murmured.

That lingering smile stretched into a grin. "I thought you'd never ask."

His jeans unfastened, revealing even more of his

amazing torso, he walked in her direction, taking his time, making each step an act of seduction.

"I...I meant it when I said I loved you."

There, she'd said it. Her heart surged higher into her throat with every step he took.

"Good." He stopped only inches away, looked down at her, then lowered his mouth to hers. The kiss lasted only seconds, not nearly long enough...just a taste of things to come. It felt like a promise...

"Because I'd sure hate to be in this alone," he murmured against her lips. "I love you, Jenn. Please don't let what I do for the Agency take you away from me."

She drew back, studying his hesitant expression. "What you do only makes me love you more." She grinned, mischief bubbling inside her. "So stop stalling. I've waited too long for this encore performance already. I have an island honeymoon on my mind."

He kissed her again, long and deep.

This time she knew it was a promise.

## Epilogue

Ethan Delaney silently watched as two men entered the dark alley on K Street in Washington, D.C.

Ethan had grown even more cautious of late, especially since Jenn had just discovered she was pregnant. They'd married in a whirlwind and parenthood was going to be the same. Ethan grinned, but he loved it…wouldn't have it any other way. Jenn's father was thrilled, as well. He'd even lit a fire under his own social life after more than a decade of being a widower. Mildred, Victoria Colby's secretary, was his latest conquest.

Ethan had taken this risk tonight for two reasons and two reasons only. He would lay down his life here and now for his employer, Victoria Colby. And he trusted Lucas Camp completely. They'd only met a couple of times, but Lucas was an old and dear friend of Victoria's. If Ethan had his guess, there was more than friendship between them, at least on Lucas's side.

Ethan stepped out of the shadows. The two men abruptly halted.

"Delaney?"

It was Lucas.

"The one and only."

Lucas continued toward him, the other man two steps behind. The older man's trademark limp was a bit more pronounced tonight than usual.

When the two entered the dim pool of light where Ethan stood, he nodded at Lucas and then looked directly at the other man.

"This is John Logan," Lucas explained. "He's one of my specialists in Mission Recovery. I'd like him on this."

Ethan considered the man. He was tall, with dark hair. He looked more than capable, a little dangerous maybe. But Ethan wasn't worried. He could be dangerous as well when necessary.

When he'd completed his visual evaluation, Ethan extended his hand. "Ethan Delaney."

Logan pumped the offered hand once, but didn't speak. That didn't particularly bother Ethan. He hadn't come here to make new acquaintances. He'd come to hear what Lucas Camp had to say. Logan was nothing more than a fixture, added protection for a middle-aged man who'd spent a lifetime making powerful enemies.

"The reason I asked for you, Delaney," Lucas began, "instead of Ian is because I know your military record. I hope we won't need your hostage retrieval skills, but I want you on this. I'd like Simon Ruhl on this, as well. We may need his old Bureau connections."

Ethan nodded. His former military life, as well as Simon's affiliation with the FBI, could definitely be beneficial at times.

"What is it that you don't want Victoria to know?"

The blunt question left Lucas silent for several moments. Whatever this was about, it couldn't be good.

Ethan had the impression Lucas never lied to Victoria. This covert meeting was telling.

"My director, Thomas Casey, is going to utilize every source he has as well. We're going to get to the bottom of this as swiftly as possible. We don't want to take any chances, but so far we don't have anything conclusive, just a few things that don't add up. Victoria mentioned to me a few weeks ago that someone in her research department had turned up some activity on a man named Leberman. I've been following up on it."

Ethan knew a tap dance when he heard one. "Look," he said pointedly. "You're going to have to be a tad more specific if you're expecting me to play along."

Lucas looked straight into Ethan's eyes. "I can't give you any specifics. I can only tell you what I believe."

Ethan waited silently through an emphatic pause.

"If Leberman is still alive and going active again, Victoria's life will be in grave danger."

Ethan considered what he knew about Leberman, Victoria's arch enemy. "And what about you?" he asked Lucas. "Doesn't that put you in the line of fire?"

"Don't worry about me, Delaney." Lucas smiled knowingly. "I have specialists like Logan here watching my back. You and the other Colby agents keep Victoria safe and I'll be happy."

Ethan nodded, acknowledging the order. "Don't worry, Mr. Camp. We won't fail Victoria."

\* \* \* \* \*

*Watch for*
LUCAS CAMP'S team of SPECIALISTS
*starting in January 2003 with*
*UNDERCOVER WIFE.*

# HARLEQUIN®
# INTRIGUE®

*A royal family in peril...*
*A kingdom in jeopardy...*
*And only love can save them!*

THE CROWN
AFFAIR

**Continues in November 2002 with**

# ROYAL RANSOM
## BY SUSAN KEARNEY

In the second exciting installment in
THE CROWN AFFAIR trilogy, Princess Tashya's baby
brothers have been kidnapped. With no time to lose,
Her Royal Highness sets out to save the young princes,
whether her family—or the dangerously seductive
CIA agent hired to protect her—liked it or not!

Coming in December 2002:
**ROYAL PURSUIT**

*Look for these exciting new stories*
*wherever Harlequin books are sold!*

# HARLEQUIN®
*Makes any time special* ®